CLASH OF MAGIC

LINSEY HALL

CHAPTER ONE

The ghost hovered over my shoulder, his anxiety crawling across my skin like ants.

"Are you sure you want to do this, Rowan?" whispered Florian, the spectral librarian. His old-fashioned English accent echoed in the dark corridors of the library. Tall shelves loomed overhead, stuffed full of old leather books that held all the secrets of the world.

I turned slightly as I walked, giving the pale ghost a determined nod. He nodded back, as if trying to prove he was on board. But it just made his tall, curly wig wobble and the lace cravat at his throat tremble. Florian Bumbledomber was the night librarian, and he hadn't changed his clothes since he'd died sometime in the eighteenth century.

"I'm sure, Florian. I have to do this. We need to know what the Stryx are, and I've found nothing in the regular part of the library. You said yourself that this was the last place to look." I shivered as a waft of cold air curled around my ankles. A pale dark mist floated over the wooden floor, and I had no idea how it had gotten there.

There were two official libraries at the Undercover Protectorate. The normal one, with warm fireplaces and cushy chairs, and the ghost library that sat behind it, past a secret entrance. The ghost library was a massive ten-story space full of millions of books. To enter it, you had to contribute something to the collection. I'd already done that ten minutes ago, and now we were deep in the bowels of the ghost library, in a wing that I'd never entered before.

"Well, you need to be careful." Florian's voice trembled. "The wraith who guards the dark collection demands a heavy price for access to his books."

"I'll pay it." I had to. I was hunting the two witches who had called themselves Stryx when I'd confronted them three days ago. I had no idea what that meant, but they had some kind of dark and deadly plan, and I needed to figure out what the heck it was.

I turned left at a tall bookshelf, heading into the depths of the library by instinct. Florian had said that my information would be in the darkest and scariest part, and that wasn't hard to identify. Since I had goose bumps on my skin and my heart was thundering, I figured I was on the right track.

"You're sure you don't want to bring someone with you?" Florian asked.

I nudged him with my arm in a friendly gesture, but my elbow passed right through him. "I brought you."

"Well, but, well..."

"And my sisters are busy." Bree and Ana were on a mission for Jude, the boss of their unit at the Undercover Protectorate. They'd be back soon, but I hadn't wanted to wait. Between my classes at the Academy and my other research into the Stryx, this was my first free moment and I'd grabbed it.

"We're almost there." Florian's voice wavered.

"You're a ghost, Florian. Why are you nervous?"

"You'll see."

A gloomy corridor loomed in front of us. It was formed by two tall bookcases that stretched back into the library. Dark mist filled it, nearly obscuring the books stacked twenty feet high. This deep in the library, the books were gray with age and dust.

"He doesn't let us come down here to dust." Florian's voice was tinged with annoyance. "Bad for the books."

The library was a labyrinth of secrets and old paper, and this right here was the darkest bit of it. Cold rolled out from the corridor, creeping up my legs to my stomach and seeping through my clothes.

I shivered and stepped toward the bookcases that formed the corridor.

"Don't!" Florian's voice cracked out. "Go no farther. Wait for him."

I stopped abruptly, swallowing hard. Florian drifted to a stop next to me, his fear palpable. I blinked into the darkness, trying to draw out any details. A dark energy filled the air, prickling against my skin like the footsteps of little spiders.

"I can't believe the Undercover Protectorate has a place like this," I whispered, a shiver crawling up my spine. "The magic is definitely dark."

"You seek dark knowledge," Florian said. "The wraith who guards this place is bound by Arach's magic, but that doesn't mean he isn't dangerous."

Arach was the dragon spirit who guarded the castle. I saw her rarely, but her power blew my socks off every time. If anyone could control the wraith, it was her. Which was good, because we were so far below the castle that no one would hear me scream.

I shook away my fear and focused on the job. Fear would get me nowhere.

The coldness increased and the dark magic swelled, stealing

the breath from my throat. The hair on my arms stood on end, and it took everything I had not to spin around and leave.

When the wraith drifted through the dark smoke filling the space between the bookshelves, I almost didn't see him. Skeletal and gaunt, he was made of the smoke itself. Only his eyes had any color, and they burned a bright, cold blue.

"What do you seek?" he hissed.

I straightened my spine. "I seek two answers and hope to find them in your collection."

"There is a price." The last syllable dragged on as if a snake had spoken the word.

"What is it?"

"A drop of blood. It must contain a bit of your energy. Your magic."

Next to me, Florian stiffened. "No. It is too dangerous."

"Of course it is," the wraith said. "You must pay a great price for knowledge."

"Will I continue to pay that price after I leave here?" I asked.

He shook his head. "Give me what I require. If you survive, you will have your information. And then you may leave, free."

I looked at Florian, who was somehow even paler than his normal ghostly form. "I'm going to do it."

He grimaced, but nodded. He knew how dangerous the Stryx were. How much I wanted to catch them.

I turned back to the wraith, who loomed closer, excitement gleaming in his eyes. "How do we do this?"

"Hold out your hand." The wraith raised his own hand, and shiny black claws tipped each long finger. They were the only solid thing on him, given that the rest of him was made of mist.

My arm trembled slightly as I raised my hand. Then I jerked it back. "Wait. I need to know that you have what I seek."

No way I was doing this if he didn't.

His irritation flowed off him, curdling in the air. "What do you seek?"

"I want to know what Stryx are. I know they're witches, but what *kind*? Where are they from? And I need a spell that will reveal a past vision shown by a Truth Teller."

Last week, I'd fought my ass off to win at a deadly obstacle course where a Truth Teller was the prize. The little charm would reveal anything you wanted to know. Unfortunately, the Stryx had beaten me to it. They'd had time to ask the Truth Teller their question, and the charm had shown them what they'd wanted to see.

I needed to know *what* it had shown them, because I was one thousand percent sure that it had to do with some dark and dangerous plan.

The wraith hesitated, then nodded. "I should have something which will help you."

"Good." Before I could back out, I thrust my hand forward.

The wraith smiled broadly, dark fangs glinting in the dim light. He raised his obsidian claw and pricked my finger with it.

Hot pain flared, greater than anything I'd ever felt. It streaked up my arm like fire, wrapping around my chest and reaching into my soul.

Through dimming vision, I caught sight of blood welling from my fingertip. My energy seemed to flow out with the blood, making my knees weak. It was as if his claw were tipped in poison.

"Such power," the wraith murmured, his words twisting through the darkness that was beginning to close in on my vision. "Such strength."

"Rowan!" Florian's voice broke through the haze of pain, and I blinked, trying desperately to stay conscious.

But it was hard. The wraith's dark magic seemed to be seeping into me, as if a connection had been formed.

Through bleary vision, I watched the wraith lick a drop of my blood off his claw. The dark magic that resided deep inside me thumped, coming to life. It was as if it recognized the wraith and wanted to say hello.

The wraith's bright blue eyes flared. "There is darkness inside you."

"There isn't." The words sounded like I'd shoved them through gravel. But they were a lie. He was right. There was darkness inside me, an evil magic that I'd shoved down so deep it hadn't seen the light in weeks. It was connected to the Stryx somehow, and it only made me more determined to stop them.

"There is." He reached out for more blood, and I yanked my hand back.

"You've had enough." It took everything I had to force down the dark magic that was welling inside me, drawn to the surface by the wraith. My body swayed forward against my will, reaching for him. Desire to get closer to him thudded within me.

I sucked in a deep breath and focused on all the good things in my life. My sisters, Maximus, the Protectorate. I wanted to keep those things, and the only way to do that was to fight the darkness that writhed within me.

Mind over matter.

I shoved every ounce of darkness away, forcing it deep down inside of me. Slowly, the pain from the wraith's magic faded as our connection broke. My vision cleared and my strength returned.

The wraith looked less skeletal now. He'd fed off my magic and my energy, using my blood as a conduit.

"I gave you what you wanted," I snapped. "Where are my answers?"

The wraith tried to glower, but his pleasure over what had just happened was too obvious. It flowed through the air, a sickly and dark energy that wrapped around me. I shivered and stepped closer to Florian.

"I'll be back." The wraith turned and drifted away, disappearing into the mist that filled the space between the shelves.

"Are you all right?" Florian asked.

"Fine."

"It seemed like I might lose you for a second there."

The darkness within me had almost overtaken me, but I wouldn't tell Florian that. "I was fine. Just shocked."

Tension thrummed across my skin as we waited for the wraith to return. When he did, he had two heavy-looking old books in his hands. I had no idea how a figure that was made of black mist was able to carry two solid books.

He handed over the smaller one, which was still at least twelve inches across. "This will contain the answer to your first question."

I took the book, shivering at the feel of dark magic that resided within it. The book's power prickled against my fingertips, making me feel like I was grabbing a cactus even though it was smooth, dusty leather.

As soon as I pulled the book toward me, it flipped open, hovering in midair. I nearly jumped, stifling a gasp as the pages flipped open, one after another. Dust motes rose high.

When the pages lay flat, I saw an illustration of a large bird.

"It looks just like the witches when they transform," I murmured, directing my words toward Florian.

Above the illustration, the word Stryx was written in a curvy script. I read quickly, my gaze racing across the page as I tried to absorb the information. I didn't know how long the wraith would give me, but his impatience was obvious as he tapped his ghostly foot.

There was very little written about them, but what I saw made my blood chill. "They're ancient Greek witches who can turn into birds. The last time anyone saw one was thousands of years ago."

"Greek?" Florian asked. "Like you?"

I swallowed hard and nodded. I wasn't Greek by birth, though I likely had some ancestors who had been. But I was the Greek DragonGod, a supernatural gifted with the powers of the Greek gods.

"We really are connected," I said. "No way they rise to power at the same time I do and there's not a connection."

I'd already *known* there was a connection, but it was somehow even scarier to see it written. To have it confirmed.

"That's enough." The wraith jerked the book back.

I bit my tongue. I'd read everything there was, so no need to snap at him and lose access to that second book. That was what I really wanted to see anyway.

The wraith passed over the heavy leather book. It was a grimoire—an ancient spell book filled with dark and dangerous magic. I didn't even need to touch it. The thing just hovered in the air in front of my chest. Golden scrollwork on the leather cover gleamed in the low light.

"Think of what you want and touch the cover," the wraith said.

As I carefully pressed my fingertips to the edge of the leather cover, I imagined a spell that would recreate what the Truth Teller had shown the Stryx. Like a revealing spell that turned back time, or something.

The cover flew open, snapping against my fingertips, and the pages began to flip so fast that they were a blur. They settled open on a page with a long list of ingredients.

Shit.

No way I could memorize all that. And if the wraith was as big a jerk as I thought he was—there was a one hundred percent chance of that—he wouldn't give me long with it. I glanced up, catching sight of his fangy smile.

Yep, this jerk was going to yank this book back soon.

Quickly, I shoved my hand in my pocket and yanked out my cell phone. It was new, and I didn't carry it often, but I'd had it on me today, thank fates. I clicked the main button on the phone twice to pull up the camera function, then raised it and snapped a quick picture.

"What are you doing?" the wraith hissed.

I snapped another picture for good measure, right before he yanked back the book. Dark magic swelled on the air, piercing my skin like wasp stings. I flinched hard.

Next to me, Florian shouted in pain.

The wraith opened his mouth wide, his fangs appearing sharp. A shriek burst from him, tearing through my head and making it ring. He raised his hands, claws pointed toward me.

Yep, I'd overstayed my welcome.

I spun on my heel and ran, sprinting through the dark library with Florian at my side. The wraith's shrieks echoed around us, shooting pain through my head. Something warm and wet trickled down my neck.

I touched it and raised my fingers up to look.

Blood. From my ears.

I shoved the cell phone back in my pocket and covered my ears as we sprinted. The black mist that surrounded us grew thicker and colder, rising up to my thighs. Suddenly, it was harder to run, as if I were trying to beat my way through a snowbank.

I slowed, my muscles burning.

"Keep going!" Florian shouted from up ahead. As a ghost, he didn't have nearly the trouble I did.

I turned to look back, catching sight of the wraith raising his hands. Behind me, bookshelves creaked, then tumbled over, collapsing inward. Heavy volumes fell from the shelves, plunging toward the ground.

Oh shit!

They were going to be damaged.

Crap, I didn't want that.

When the books neared the ground, they stopped abruptly, floating in midair. Then they moved, hurtling toward me.

Oh, double shit!

I turned and ran, trying to outrun the heavy volumes that charged toward me. There were hundreds of them, and if they reached me, they'd crush me.

The fog dragged at my legs, making every muscle burn, but I pushed harder. My breath heaved as I raced past the book-shelves.

A heavy book hit me in the back, and I nearly stumbled forward. Another hit me on the arm, then one on the thigh. Pain flared each time, the beginning of a deep bruise.

We were coming up to a long row of tables stretching toward the wide, sweeping staircase that led to the exit. I neared the first table and leapt, then scrambled up onto the heavy wooden surface. It was above the low-lying fog that pulled at my legs. Up here, I could run faster.

I sprinted ahead as the books raced after me, sparing a brief glance behind me and spotting hundreds of volumes chasing me.

My heart thundered hard. They formed a solid wall, and they were nearly to me.

I turned back and sprinted as fast as I could.

"Hurry!" Florian shouted. He waved me on from up ahead, his eyes bright and his wig askew.

I leapt from table to table, the cold mist grabbing for my feet.

"Nearly there!" Florian turned and sprinted up the stairs to the main part of the ghost library.

Lungs heaving and muscles burning, I joined him, leaping onto the wide staircase and following him up. I took the stairs three at a time, moving faster than I ever had in my life. We reached the next level and I turned.

The books had stopped at the bottom, hovering menacingly in the air.

Panting, Florian propped his hands on his knees. "They can't come here. The rest of the ghost library is out of the wraith's control."

"Thank fates." I leaned against the bannister and surveyed the rest of the library. It was a massive, ten-story affair with a huge open atrium in the middle that led all the way up to the domed skylight. Each level of the library was a circle surrounding the atrium.

"Let's go," Florian said. "I don't want to test that theory."

"Couldn't agree more." I followed him up the stairs, ascending five flights to the middle of the ghost library where it joined with the main library.

We slipped through a narrow door in the shelves, emerging into the warmth and color of the main library.

Immediately, the prickly chill that had enveloped me disappeared. Unlike the ghost library, which was round, this room was a tall, massive rectangle. The books were well cared for and gleamed with colorful leather spines. Four massive fireplaces crackled merrily, sharing their warmth with fat, cozy armchairs.

The Pugs of Destruction, three ghostly inhabitants of the castle, snoozed away in front of one of the fires.

I collapsed into one of the chairs next to Florian, my muscles shaking from the adrenaline high.

"Did you get what you came for?" Florian asked.

With a trembling hand, I withdrew the phone from my pocket. "I hope so."

I clicked the buttons, pulling up the photo and squinting at

11

it. The image was a bit fuzzy, but I could read it all. "Oh, thank fates."

"You have it." There was a smile in Florian's voice. "Quick thinking with your little gadget there. That page was too long to memorize."

"No kidding." I inspected the list of ingredients in the spell. I recognized almost all of them, but there was one that was unfamiliar. "What's a Veil of Power?"

Florian frowned. "It wants a Veil of Power? Those are quite rare."

"Do we have one here?"

"We do, I believe. But for you to obtain access to it, as a student..." He shook his head. "That is unlikely."

"I'll just have to convince Jude that I need it."

A doubtful frown tugged at the corners of his mouth. "Do you think you can?"

"I'm going to have to."

CHAPTER TWO

"So, I was hoping that I could have access to the Veil of Power. I need it for a spell that will tell me what the Stryx are up to." I gave Jude a hopeful look. It was just one ingredient in the spell, but it was vital.

Her starry blue eyes narrowed as she thought, her smooth dark brow creasing. The braids that hung down her back glinted in the light of the sconces. I'd cornered her right before class and spelled out what had happened down at the bottom of the ghost library.

"You went to see the wraith at the bottom of the library by yourself?" Her scowl deepened.

I nodded tentatively. True, it was against the rules and I'd known it when I'd done it, but I'd *had* to. "I had Florian."

"You know he doesn't count."

"You're right. I knew it was a risk, but I had to take it. I've looked everywhere else in the library for answers and found none. And you know how dangerous the Stryx are."

They'd killed people. Lots of people. And now they were up to something even darker. I was sure of it.

Jude gave a long-suffering sigh. "I know they're dangerous. Just like I know the wraith is dangerous."

"This is bigger than all of us, Jude."

"I know it is. And you've proven yourself capable ever since you started at the Protectorate. More than capable."

"So I can use the Veil of Power?"

Jude squinted down at my cell phone, which she held in her hand. Her gaze traveled over the words on the screen. "I think you're going to *have* to be the one to use the Veil of Power. This spell requires so much raw magic that you and your sisters are some of the few with the strength." Her gaze flicked up to mine. "Do you think you're ready for this?"

"Yes." I nodded firmly. I *needed* to be ready for this. The Stryx were forging ahead with their plans. They wouldn't wait for me and my wonky magic to catch up.

"Fine. You can use the Veil of Power. As long as you do so with Hedy's supervision."

"Of course." I grinned. It was better that way, actually. Hedy was our resident Research & Development witch, and easily the most accomplished spell worker at the Undercover Protectorate. We needed for this spell to go right, and her help would be invaluable.

"You'll conduct the spell as part of class," Jude said. "It can be part of one of the lessons."

I swallowed hard. *In class?*

That meant in front of an audience. An audience of people I didn't really like. And who definitely didn't like me.

But what choice did I have? I nodded. "Okay. How about in this class, since we're down here in the spell room anyway?"

At least that way, I could get it over with quickly. And I wanted my answers ASAP.

"That's exactly what I was thinking."

The stone-walled room on the castle's bottom floor was

where all the spellwork classes were conducted, largely because the walls were thick and heavy enough to keep any wayward magic from hurting the rest of the castle. We didn't have these classes often, and I didn't want to wait to figure out what the Stryx had learned from the Truth Teller. Since a class was starting in twenty minutes, there was no need to wait.

"I'll bring the Veil of Power to class." Jude gave me a serious look. "Be sure you're ready to try this, because it won't be an easy spell. It will take a lot of your magic to accomplish."

The first tendrils of nerves crept over my spine. *A lot of my magic.*

I did have a lot of magic.

What I didn't have was a lot of control over it. I'd been getting new powers from the Greek gods, and to say that there was a learning curve was an understatement. I had lightning power from Zeus and water magic from Poseidon, but it was my strange death magic that scared the crap out of me. I had to assume it was a gift from Hades, and it gave me the ability to suck the life from plants and use it as my own.

But it was just so...*dark.*

I was resisting practicing it, and I knew it was dumb, but I couldn't help myself. With the Rebel Gods' dark magic stuffed down deep inside me, I didn't want to do anything to wake it.

"I can do it, Jude," I said. "You don't have to worry about me."

I saw no skepticism in her face, which warmed me slightly.

While Jude went to speak to Hedy about the Veil of Power, I hurried back to my apartment to grab the Truth Teller. I'd won it in the Intermagic Games obstacle course a few days ago. Unfortunately, the Stryx had immediately stolen it from me and used it. There'd been a hell of a fight to get it back. They'd managed to get information from it first, though, and that was what I needed to figure out with the Veil of Power.

As for the Truth Teller, I'd had a few days with it myself to ask it questions and try to figure out what the Stryx were up to. Soon, I'd give it to the Protectorate so they could use it in their work to help people.

By the time I made it back down to the classroom, the other students were in place. They sat at long, heavy wooden tables, all of them clustered together. Lavender glared at me, and I returned the favor, shooting my archnemesis a scowl.

In fairness, I didn't dislike her that much. I had real problems and real enemies, and Lavender didn't figure into that. She might make my life in class hell, but we were still on the same team. I could appreciate that, at least. But it was kind of fun to pretend I had an archnemesis.

I sat at a long table near the other students, my gaze glued to the big table at the front of the room. That was where demonstrations were done. No doubt I'd go up there to cast my own spell.

The room was large, the walls made of huge heavy stones. The vaulted ceiling was also made of stone, and I had one quick, horrible vision of my magic going awry and ricocheting wildly around the room.

I shook away the thought.

Nope. I had this under control. I could do this.

Jude swept into the room a moment later, a small wooden box in her hand. My heart leapt as my gaze zeroed in on it. That was it. It had to be.

Hedy followed her into the room, her lavender hair flowing behind her and her colorful skirts swishing around her legs. She took a seat near the front while Jude headed up to the main table and set the box down. She didn't mention it, just started up with class as if everything were normal.

We were discussing proper technique when performing unfamiliar spells. Jude explained that our assignment was to replicate a spell from a spell book. Lavender and Angus went first, and I barely registered what they were doing.

Frankly, it was all a blur. By the time it was my turn, tension vibrated through my muscles.

Jude's gaze found mine. "Rowan, it's your turn."

I stood, reaching into my pocket for my cell phone. Excitement and nerves thrummed through me as I headed to the front of the class. I focused most of my time at the Academy on combat and tracking, so this was unusual. I hadn't always been great at spellwork, but with so much on the line, I was determined to change my record.

Hedy joined me at the table, and I heard Lavender snicker. "She needs a supervisor."

Jude didn't seem to hear her, and I was grateful. I didn't need my future boss knowing that I was having a spat with my colleague. And the last thing I wanted was anyone defending me.

I fought my own battles, thanks.

I looked at the class, feeling the weight of their gazes. "I'm going to be conducting a spell that reveals what the Truth Teller showed to a person who used it last."

The crowd stared at me, slightly dumbfounded. They weren't quite up to date on all that had been happening with the Stryx, and I wasn't about to enlighten them. I just had to get my answers.

I pulled the Truth Teller from my pocket and set the small stone on the table. It gleamed golden in the light, a tiny object that held so many answers. Unfortunately, it wasn't always easy to get those answers *out*.

Next, I pulled up the spell on my phone and set it on the table. Hedy leaned over my shoulder and peered at it.

"Won't be easy," she murmured. "Though there's a lot of

ingredients here, it relies mostly on raw power. Without it, the spell won't work."

That wasn't great. I was a wizard with potions ingredients. Not so much with my raw magic, unfortunately.

This time, though, I'd get it right.

I had to.

The box containing the Veil of Power buzzed with magic. I could almost see the wood vibrating. I picked it up and opened it, then removed a lacy little cloth that looked like it'd been spun by spiders. Magic prickled against my fingertips, feeling like popping champagne bubbles.

Carefully, I laid the veil over the Truth Teller. At her seat, Lavender leaned over and whispered to Angus. I ignored her, focusing on the tiny text on my phone. There were a few ingredients I had to mix before I could start the incantation.

Working quickly, I picked up the proper vials and poured tiny droplets into an onyx bowl. The liquid smoked as it hit the stone.

"This is taking forever," Lavender whispered.

I scowled. If Jude reprimanded her, I didn't hear it. I was too focused on the task at hand. Each measurement of the various ingredients had to be perfect. If I so much as trembled, this would fail.

Finally, the potion was mixed. It smoked lightly, smelling of lilacs and burning tires—a weird combo.

I glanced at Hedy, the question clear in my eyes. *Did I get this right?*

"You're doing well," Hedy murmured.

That was because we hadn't reached the hard part yet.

I drew in a deep breath and held the potion over the veil. Carefully, I poured the liquid onto the lace, which flared a bright gold. Magic burst from it, a wave of power that blew my hair back from my face.

As quickly as I could, I put down the onyx bowl and touched the little stone with both hands. I fed my magic into the rock, acting as a battery for the spell. It flowed from me, through the veil, and into the stone. It all combined to form something greater, something more powerful than the sum of the ingredients.

"That's it," Hedy murmured. "Keep going. It's going to need more than that."

I reached for the magic deep inside me, feeding it into the lacy cloth that was soaked in potion. This was where it got tricky. I had magic on the surface that was easy to control. But the bulk of my power resided deep inside me. It was a mix of my own power, the power from the Greek gods, and a bit of the darkness from the Rebel Gods who'd held me prisoner for years.

I couldn't put the dark stuff into this spell, so I focused on drawing out only the light. When I tried to take the magic that Zeus had given me—the crackling lightning—it snapped and burned inside me. I stayed far away from Hades's magic.

Shaking, I fed the power into the veil. Sweat dripped down my spine, and my muscles ached. I squeezed my eyes shut and focused, trying to keep my grip on the magic, feeding it in a steady stream. It thrashed inside me, wanting to burst out in a powerful blast.

Lightning was not an easily controlled substance, that was for sure.

"Careful," Hedy murmured, clearly able to sense that I was losing control.

My arms shook as I tried to keep it together, using every bit of strength and will not to blow it entirely.

"That's it," Hedy said. "You're getting it."

I opened my eyes to see a haze of smoke forming above the stone. It coalesced to form an image, just like it had when the Stryx had first used it. I'd caught the barest glance of it then, but had only been able to decipher a vision of mountains and lightning.

Now, I could see a blazing red sunset and hear explosions. The mountain was black, formed of volcanic rubble. At least, that's what I thought I was seeing. I squinted, trying to make out the details.

Every inch of me ached as I fed more magic into the spell, powering the potion and the veil so that they could do their work. Weakness sucked at my limbs, exhaustion pulling at my mind. The lightning within me cracked and burst, trying to break free of the carefully controlled stream that I was feeding into the veil.

My muscles trembled uncontrollably.

"Rowan, you're weakening." Concern echoed in Hedy's voice. "Perhaps you should slow down."

Slow down? We were so close! The image projected by the Truth Teller and the veil was growing more detailed. We had to see more!

I ignored her words, pushing more of my magic into the spell. Sweat dripped down my temple.

"Rowan, stop."

But I couldn't. I needed to see. I needed to stop the Stryx. I knew deep in my heart that they were up to something that would hurt thousands. Millions.

But my magic was so hard to control. It took everything I had.

But it wasn't enough.

The power burst out of me, a lightning bolt that shot to the ceiling. It ricocheted off, just as I'd imagined, and slammed toward the ground, hitting the tables where the other students sat. They flew backward, screams breaking through the quiet room.

I stumbled away from the Truth Teller, a gasp tearing from

my throat. The magic inside me died down, the pressure released.

Wild-eyed, I looked toward the Truth Teller. The vision had faded.

Damn it.

I looked up, catching sight of Jude's gaze.

Oh, shit.

She looked pissed.

In the middle of the room, the other students were rising to their feet, glaring at me.

"You've done it now," Hedy murmured, sympathy in her gaze.

"Yep."

She squeezed my arm. "You did well until the end."

"Thanks." Dread coiled inside me as Jude helped the class fix the overturned tables and chairs, then dismissed them.

I tried to ignore what was going on, instead focusing my attention on cleaning up the supplies I'd used. I created neat little rows of potion bottles and packed the Veil of Power away in its box. The scrap of lace looked tattered and ratty now, as if the surge of my power had damaged it.

Jude approached the table, her starry blue eyes serious. "You didn't listen to Hedy when she told you to stop."

I just nodded. There was nothing I could say. I *had* ignored Hedy. The results were obvious. There was a giant freaking divot in the ceiling that was burned black from my lightning.

"You need to get control of your magic, Rowan. These new gifts from the gods aren't resting easily inside of you."

She was right on that, and I suspected it might be because of the dark magic in my soul. I might have repressed it, but it was still hanging out alongside the good magic. The result was less than desirable.

"I'll get it under control," I said.

"Maximus has been busy with the Order, as I'm sure you may know, but he'll return to help train you next week."

I nodded, trying to keep my cheeks from flaring red. Maximus, the powerful gladiator mage whom I definitely had some feelings for, had been away from the Protectorate the last few days. He was a freelancer with the Order of the Magica and the Undercover Protectorate both, a difficult position given that I had magic that the Order would love to see me thrown in prison for possessing.

Maximus kept my secret, thank fates. It was easy for him, since he was so wealthy it didn't matter if the Order fired him.

As much as I could probably use his help getting my power under control, I also wanted to see him. I liked him, damn it. More than I should.

"Until you've got your magic together, I'm not sure that you should practice around the other students," Jude said.

My heart plummeted. The only way to join the PITs—the Paranormal Investigative Team where my sisters worked—was to pass the Academy. If I couldn't go to class, I couldn't pass.

Shit.

"It's a matter of safety," Jude said. "You're the most accomplished student here, when things go well. When they don't..."

"I'm a danger." I finished the sentence for her, unable to help myself. For all the good things I'd accomplished, there were still some messy areas of my life.

Like the fact that lightning now exploded out of me occasionally.

Not great.

"It's more than that," Hedy said. "Your magic isn't united within you. Your lack of control isn't just a danger to others. It's a danger to you."

"What do you mean?"

"We've seen this before," Hedy said. "With your sister Bree. If you can't get your magic under control—and *soon*—it will devour you from the inside. You'll become the walking dead. A shell of yourself. Just a husk with no soul and no magic."

I swallowed hard, ice streaking through my veins. I'd known this was a vague possibility, but hadn't really thought it would happen to me.

I'd ignored it.

But it was happening, apparently. Right now.

"How long do I have?" I asked.

Hedy's gaze turned serious. "I don't know. A couple weeks? Maybe a bit longer? It all depends on your power, Rowan. And you."

CHAPTER THREE

A few hours later, after a shower to get the smell of burnt ozone off of me, I found my sisters at the Whiskey and Warlock. The little pub was almost empty since it wasn't yet five in the evening. The scarred old tables and chairs gleamed a warm golden wood, and copper mugs hung from the ceiling.

Bree and Ana were the only ones in the little room where the Protectorate usually gathered. They sat at a small table near the roaring fire, each with a drink in front of them. Bree's pink cocktail shined in the light, while Ana's pink champagne bubbled away.

The sight of them, a bit worn and mussed-looking from their recent job, warmed my insides. I turned from them and faced the bar, leaning on the gleaming wood. Sophie, the bartender, turned to smile at me. Today, her shirt said *Mess with Nessie and You Mess with Me.*

"What'll it be?" she asked.

"Tea, please. Just a bit of milk."

"No beer?"

I shook my head. "Can't say that I deserve it today."

I needed to get to practicing my magic, but I'd wanted to see Bree and Ana first.

"I doubt that's true," Sophie said.

"Kinda is."

I guess my face said it all, because she just nodded sympathetically and went to the back to brew some tea. "Take a seat and I'll bring it out." Her voice echoed from the kitchen.

"Thanks," I shouted, then went to join my sisters. I smiled at them, nodding to their drinks. "You're starting early."

"Celebrating." Bree grinned widely, shoving her dark hair back from her cheek. "We caught the Melphius demon who's been terrorizing Pitlochry."

"Really?" I'd been hearing about how the hellbeast was burning houses and catching people as they fled the flames. "Then you deserve a celebratory drink."

At that moment, I wanted to be them. To have finished with my classes and proven myself worthy. To have joined the team and my sisters at the Protectorate, fighting to keep people safe.

Ana nodded, her blonde hair glinting in the light of the flames. "It wasn't easy, but we took him down."

At her arm, a wound bled sluggishly. I scowled at her. "Let me take care of that."

"What?" She glanced down. "Oh, that. I hardly noticed. There were worse ones."

"So you've already done some healing?" I frowned, not liking the idea that she'd been worse off than this.

"A *lot* of it." She sipped her pink bubbles and sighed happily. "I'm pretty much tapped out now, but that one's little. It's fine."

"Well, let me see to this anyway." I pulled a little vial of healing potion from my belt and dabbed it on the wound. While I worked, Sophie delivered my tea.

"Just tea for you?" Ana asked as I put the vial of potion back in my belt.

"Got a problem."

They both leaned forward, their eyes concerned. As if they were the same person, they spoke in unison. "It's your magic, isn't it?"

I swallowed hard and nodded, explaining how my new lightning magic was exploding out of me. I'd had pretty good control of the water power I'd first gotten from the gods, but now that I had another power, it was all going haywire inside me. Not to mention Hades's magic...

"Oh no." Bree's face paled. "I was worried about this. You need to get it under control."

"Fast," Ana said.

"I know."

"We always knew this was a risk. But I didn't really believe it would happen to you." Bree shook her head. "Probably because I didn't want to face it."

"We can help you get it under control," Ana said. "So can Maximus. He's very skilled."

Just the thought of Maximus made me warm inside. I shoved it away and reached for her hand. "Thanks, guys."

"Of course. We're always here for you," Bree said. "I can help you with your lightning power."

"I'm not bad with the elements," Ana said. "Water is a specialty of mine."

"But what about that power from Hades?" Bree asked. "The one that lets you suck the life from plants."

I blanched. "Um, that one is tough."

"Have you practiced with it?" Bree asked.

"No."

"You have to," Ana said.

"I don't want it," I said. In fact, I was pretty damned scared of it. I loathed admitting that, though, even to myself.

"It doesn't matter if you want it," Bree said. "You need to

make it work for you. That's probably part of your problem. You can't ignore it."

"I know. You're right." I leaned forward. "I also got a hint of what the Stryx saw in the Truth Teller, before my magic blew up and caused problems."

Bree leaned in. "Really? What?"

I described the blazing sky and black mountains, the explosions. Before I finished, a noise blared from the comms charm around Ana's neck, sharp and loud. The three of us jumped.

My heart thundered. "What the hell is that?"

"Red alert." Ana pressed her fingertips to her comms charm, igniting the magic within it. "Jude? What is it?"

"Emergency in northern Greece." She rattled off a list of geographical coordinates. "Get here soon. Be prepared to climb, and watch out for the Obsidia. Mean little bastards."

"What?" Confusion echoed in Ana's voice, but there was the sound of an explosion, then the connection cut out. "Jude? Jude!"

There was no response.

They surged to their feet and I followed.

"We've got to go," Bree said.

"I'm coming." I stepped forward.

"You don't have to," Ana says. "It could be dangerous."

"From the sound of that explosion, it *is* dangerous," I said. "I'm coming anyway. It's in Greece. I'm the Greek DragonGod. No way I'm not coming."

Bree shot Ana a look. "She has a point."

I grinned. "Exactly."

Ana nodded. "Let's get a move on, then."

We hurried out onto the street, which had already grown dark.

Bree reached into her pocket and withdrew a transport charm. "I'll get us as close as I can to those coordinates."

Ana and I nodded, and she hurled the transport charm to the ground. It exploded upward in a cloud of glittery black dust, and the three of us stepped into it.

The ether sucked me in and spun me around, spitting me out into the middle of what felt like a war zone. I coughed and stumbled on gravel. Smoke burned my eyes as I looked around.

We stood in a valley between two huge black hills, the earth itself made of crumbly black rocks. The sun was beginning to set, shedding an eerie, pale light over the smoke that drifted down from the top of one of the hills. The sound of explosions echoed in the distance, but I couldn't see them yet.

"Where are we?" I scraped my hair off my face and turned in a circle, looking for clues.

"Besides Greece? No idea." Bree's silver wings flared from her back, and she launched herself into the air. "Going for recon. Be back soon."

She flew high into the smoky sky. Ana and I looked up, following her progress. The air here stank of sulfur and burning stuff. In all the pictures I'd seen of Greece, I'd never seen anything like these massive black hills.

Dark magic prickled in the air, a powerful force that made my skin crawl and my senses go on high alert.

"Something is *really* wrong here," I said.

"No kidding." Ana pointed toward the sky. "Here she comes."

Bree appeared through the smoke, her silver wings bright against the dark clouds. She landed next to us, her face streaked with soot. "I couldn't see much, but I think we have to head up that hill."

She pointed to the one that was belching smoke. I nodded and trudged toward it, the glassy gravel easily swallowing my boots up to my ankles.

"Do we know who else is up there?" I shouted through the sound of explosions.

28

"I couldn't see anyone," Bree said.

I tried to breathe shallowly to keep the smoke out of my lungs, but it wasn't working. It burned as I climbed, my muscles aching in tandem. All around, the gravel shifted, flowing downward as something at the top of the mountain disturbed it.

"Do you hear that?" Bree asked, tipping her head to the left.

"No." I tried, but I couldn't. Bree had godly hearing, though. A gift from Heimdall, a Norse god.

"Something is stalking us."

The words made a chill race down my spine.

Something is stalking us. That was the last thing you ever wanted to hear.

I didn't have my potion bombs since I hadn't brought my bag, but I did have my dagger and some other weapons stored in the ether. Also my magic, but that was totally wonky and I wasn't sure I wanted to risk it.

"To the left," Ana said.

I glanced over, spotting a flash of movement against the black ground. The figure was only a few feet tall and blade-like, each limb as skinny as a sword. And if I wasn't mistaken, the creature was made of black glass. Red eyes gleamed at us.

"That must be the Obsidia," I said.

"Ten bucks it's made of obsidian," Bree said.

"Not taking that bet." I was certain it was made of the black volcanic glass. Unfortunately for us, obsidian was the sharpest surface on earth. Brittle, though, thank fates.

We continued to hurry up the mountain, keeping our pace quick and our gazes on the Obsidia. By the time we'd climbed another hundred yards, there were three Obsidias. Then four. They didn't have faces—just red eyes on a jagged slab of black volcanic glass that protruded upward from the shoulders.

The sounds of explosions intensified, covering up the skittering noise that the Obsidias made when they moved.

"They're getting closer," Ana said.

She was right. The little jerks were creeping ever closer, their blade-like arms outstretched toward us. They had no fingers or hands, just glassy swords for limbs, which were longer than their legs. Easily a three-foot reach. That was a heck of a lot longer than my sword, and definitely long enough to do some serious damage.

Heart pounding, I moved my hand toward my side, out of view of the Obsidias. Then I called my sword from the ether, preparing for an attack.

As a group, the beasts charged, all four of them racing across the gravelly slope toward us. Their red eyes flamed and their glassy bodies gleamed.

Bree launched herself into the air, drawing a long sword from the ether. She shot toward the little monsters, her blade raised. As soon as she hovered above it, the creature jumped, launching itself fifteen feet into the air and slicing out with its arm.

Bree shrieked and dodged, diving aside just in time to avoid a nasty cut. The Obsidia landed on the ground, then leapt up again, flying twenty feet high this time. Bree was ready for him, though, and she struck out with her blade, shattering the creature's arm.

The little monster didn't so much as flinch, though I wasn't surprised. Dark magic reeked from them, stinking of sulfur and death. They were dark magic creatures, built of magic and stone instead of flesh and bone. Pain wouldn't be something they were familiar with.

Beside me, Ana raised her hands, her magic swelling on the air. She used her power over the earth, calling upon the gravelly ground to rise up and slam into two of the beasts who were closest to us. They flew backward, buried under a pile of tiny rocks.

I lunged for a creature that charged us, my blade raised high. The monster charged at me, jumping ten feet to sail through the air, headed right for my head. Before it reached me, I swiped out with my blade, shattering the creature's arm. Black glass shards flew everywhere, tiny pieces slicing across my cheek and neck.

The Obsidia landed gracefully and spun, swiping out with its other arm, aiming at my leg. I darted out of the way, but too slowly. The glass cut through my shin, and pain flared.

I gritted my teeth and dived forward, slicing through the Obsidia's body with my sword. As the creature shattered, I threw my arm up in front of my face, covering my skin. Glass shards embedded themselves in my jacket, but I escaped the worst of it.

When I lowered my arm, I spotted Bree and Ana tag teaming three more Obsidia. Ana kept them distracted with sprays of gravel while Bree attacked with her sword from the sky. They took them out one by one, and I turned my attention to scanning our surroundings, searching for more attackers.

The wound at my shin burned, but I ignored it. When a shift in the rubble to my left caught my eye, I tightened my grip on my blade.

A half second later, an Obsidia burst from the ground, red eyes blazing. Its gaze glued to me, and it charged, razor-sharp arms outstretched.

I sprinted toward the monster. It was comforting, having a problem that I could fix with just my blade and muscles.

As I neared the Obsidia, I swiped out with my blade and slammed it into the creature's arms. They shattered, but the beast used the stub of one to slice at my arm. He made contact, and agony flared, making my eyes water and a cry tear from my throat.

Thank fates it isn't my sword arm.

I raised my blade and brought it down across the creature's chest, shattering him into a hundred pieces. I was too slow to

31

cover my face, and the glass bit in sharply, a dozen pinpricks of pain.

When I lowered my arm, I spotted my sisters. Bree had landed next to Ana.

The monsters were gone.

"You okay?" I shouted over the sound of explosions.

Ana bled from her arm and Bree from her leg, but they both looked all right.

"Just dandy!" Ana said.

"Couldn't be better." Bree grinned.

Ana turned to Bree, her hand glowing golden with her healing light. "Let me take care of that leg."

While they healed up with Ana's Druid healing power, I pulled a healing potion from my belt. This one was meant to be drunk, and it'd be better for the gashes and tiny wounds. I took a sparing sip, wanting to save some for later, and felt the pain begin to fade.

A few tiny glass shards fell from my face as my skin evicted them in the healing process. Once I was sure they were all gone, I did my best to wipe the blood away.

All healed up, we continued to climb toward the top. Every inch of me prickled with awareness as I kept my senses tuned for more Obsidia.

As we climbed, the sound of explosions grew louder. The earth beneath my feet shook, and more rubble flowed down the hillside. It took everything I had to stay on my feet, and I struggled to keep upright.

By the time Jude's figure appeared at the top of the hill, surrounded by the blaze of the setting sun, all of my muscles were burning. I wiped the sweat away from my face and peered at her.

Behind her tall figure, there were more hills. Gravel and smoke exploded upward, revealing a silhouette of horror.

I gasped at the familiar sight, stumbling backward. The strongest sense of déjà vu swept over me, highlighting all the similarities between this scene and the one shown to me by the Truth Teller.

"We're here." The words came out in a rush.

"What?" Bree asked.

"This. This scene is what the Truth Teller showed the Stryx." I turned to my sisters, knowing my eyes had to be wild.

Ana and Bree's eyes widened.

"The red sky and black mountains," Bree said.

"The explosions." Ana covered her ears as a particularly violent one struck.

"What's going on?" Jude shouted, climbing down the mountain toward us, her braids blowing in the wind.

I turned to face her. "This looks just like the scene that the Truth Teller showed me in class." I pointed to the explosions. "This is the work of the Stryx."

Jude's eyes narrowed. "Really? I got a glimpse of red in the image, but didn't see it well."

"Really. I saw it so clearly."

She waved us forward. "Then come up and check it out closer. See if you still feel the same when you get to the top."

I scrambled up the hillside behind her, moving as quickly as I could. By the time I reached the top, I realized it was a massive crater. We were standing on the spoils of a huge digging operation. In the pit below, the Stryx were plowing into the earth using explosives. We were near a volcano—we had to be, given all the obsidian flying through the air—and the Stryx were just going deeper.

I squinted down into the middle of the gigantic crater, but I could see nothing except smoke and explosions.

"We can't get in!" Jude shouted over the noise. "We've tried, but there is a barrier blocking us."

"So you can't stop them?" I asked.

"Not yet."

"It's definitely the Stryx, though. I'd bet my life on it."

"Good." Jude nodded. "At least we know, now."

I turned back toward the explosions, finally spotting Maximus standing about thirty yards away on the same ridge. He looked tall and strong enough to break a bus in half. His arms were crossed over his chest and his face creased in a scowl as he watched the explosions. He hadn't seen me yet.

"Why is he here?" I asked.

"Sent by the Order," Jude said. "This is serious. If the Stryx keep this up for much longer, all the rocks that they're blowing out of the earth are going to crush a nearby village."

My stomach plunged.

"Oh, fates," Bree murmured. "Human or supernatural?"

"Both."

She frowned. "So we can't even tell them the truth. We have to protect them without revealing there's magic."

"And that's a hell of a lot harder," Jude said.

I stared at the explosions below, horror and fear rising within me like a thick black tar. "You don't know what they are after?"

"Not a clue," Jude said. "We only know it's the Stryx because you say so."

I turned to her. "Do you believe me?"

"I believe that you believe it." She shrugged. "And I trust you. So yes, right now, we'll assume it is the Stryx. But what they're doing, I have no idea."

I turned back to the explosions, trying to see through the thick black smoke that surrounded the Stryx's operation. The longer I looked at it, the more powerful it felt. The magic within the crater grew, calling to me.

I stepped backward, shaking my head and sucking in a breath.

That was weird.

I tried to look away, to find my sisters or Maximus. But I couldn't. My gaze was glued on the smoky crater. The magic within rose up toward me, twisting around my body and seeping inside my skin.

Come.

The voice echoed in my ears, impossible to ignore.

Come to us.

I shook my head, resisting. But the magic within the crater called. Worse, it *pulled*. As if the tendrils of dark magic had twisted around my muscles and bones, it had a grip on me. It tugged me forward.

Part of me wanted to go. Wanted to figure out what was happening down there.

Most of me knew it was a death wish.

The magic didn't care what I wanted. It tugged me forward, forcing my limbs to move. Panic flared in my chest. I struggled against the magic's hold, trying to pull myself back and fight the grip of the dark power.

Come to us.

Against my will, I walked forward, my muscles forced into action. I tried to scream, but no sound escaped my lips. My body was a prisoner to the magic, and I was stumbling down the hill toward the smoke below.

"No!" I tried to scream, but the words were just a whisper.

Out of the corner of my eye, I caught sight of three tiny figures.

The Menacing Menagerie. Drawn here by my distress, no doubt. The three little creatures clung to my legs, trying to hold me back. They weren't strong enough, though, and I stumbled forward like a zombie.

Did my sisters not see me? Jude or Maximus?

I was walking to my death, forced by this dark magic, and they hadn't noticed.

My heart thundered in my ears, nearly deafening.

"Rowan!" Maximus's shout echoed with fear. "Stop!"

But I couldn't. Finally, he'd seen me, but I was so far down.

"Rowan!" my sisters screamed in unison, but their voices echoed in the distance. They were too far.

I was too far.

Then I was enveloped in the darkness entirely. Their voices were gone. My breath was gone. My will was gone. I kept walking, straight through the thick black fog and toward the explosions that made every bone in my body shake.

Without a doubt, I knew the truth.

I would die here.

CHAPTER FOUR

The Stryx's evil magic pulled me deep into the darkness. All around, the explosions shook the air. Shook the ground. Only magic kept me upright, but I fought it anyway, trying to escape the grip of the Stryx. They were calling me to them, and if they got ahold of me, I was dead.

The Menacing Menagerie were gone, no doubt forced away by this evil power.

What kind of magic could do this?

When a golden light blared through the darkness, it was like a breath of air to a drowning person. Something grabbed me—a hand, tight around my arm. It yanked me backward, strong and sure.

I stumbled, breaking away from the pull of the Stryx. The hand that had grabbed me belonged to someone with great power. Golden magic, strong and bright. The figure pulled me from the black smoke.

Once the magic had loosened its grip on me, I coughed and spun. I stood within a golden circle, a clearing in the middle of the smoke.

In front of me, Hermes stood. The messenger god wore his

winged sandals and a golden helmet. His skin and white tunic were stained with the smoke around us, and his brow was creased with worry.

"What happened?" I shouted over the sound of explosions. "Where are we?"

"A protective circle." Hermes coughed, using his tunic to cover his mouth so he could breathe. "The Stryx dragged you in. They want you."

I shivered, eyeing the darkness that surrounded us. "Why?"

"They need you. For what, I do not know. But you must not go to them. Your goal must be to defeat them."

"I wasn't trying to go to them. Something dragged me toward them. They've never been able to do that before."

"They are powerful. More powerful than you have seen." Strain creased his brow. "Even now, it is difficult for me to keep you safe from them."

"Why did you save me?"

"Queens Hippolyta and Penthesilea demanded that I do so. I owe them a favor."

"Who the hell are they?" The smoke was starting to make it hard to breathe.

"The Amazons, the greatest warriors in Greek history."

My jaw nearly dropped. "They're real?"

He gave me a look that suggested I was an idiot.

He wasn't totally off the mark, actually. If Hermes, the messenger god, existed, of course the Amazons existed.

"Why do they care about me?" I asked.

"They wish to see you. And not only that—*you* need to see *them*. Your magic is not settling well within you—it is fractured. If you are lucky, this journey will help you fix that." His gaze turned dark. "But it must be soon, before it is too late. Before the magic devours you. Your magic, your soul."

I swallowed hard. "Devours me?"

"The fate of a DragonGod is not an easy one, and the Greek gods have gifted you with such great power that you must work hard to control it. You don't have much time left. Perhaps a week?"

I swallowed hard. Less time than I'd thought. "Where do I find the Amazons?" I wracked my mind for any memory of the great warrior women. "Don't they live on an island somewhere?"

"That is fiction. They once lived along the shore of the Black Sea. In the modern day, they have adapted. You will find them in Istanbul. Search for the symbol of the warrior woman, and you will find them." He reached for my hand and pressed something into it. A stone. "That transport charm will take you to them."

"What do I do once I find them?"

"Whatever they tell you to. If you're lucky, you'll learn to control your magic. You might also learn how to stop the Stryx. They're connected to you, Rowan. You must get control of your magic to have any hope of defeating them."

"So I might figure out what they are up to?"

"Yes, if you survive."

A pulse of power from the darkness nearly bowled me over. Even Hermes stumbled.

His face paled. "I must go. It is becoming too dangerous."

Before I could speak, he grabbed my arm and pulled me through the smoky air. For the briefest moment, it threatened to suck me back in and drag me toward the Stryx. But Hermes kept his grip firm.

When we stumbled out onto the mountainside, the orange light of the nearly setting sun blinded me. Hermes disappeared immediately, and I spun in a circle, searching for my friends.

Explosions still sounded from within the crater, and dark debris flew into the sky. About twenty feet down the slope into the crater, my friends looked as if they were banging on an invisible wall, trying to push their way through. Maximus, Bree, and

Ana fought like mad, punching and kicking the wall. Jude looked like she was trying to funnel glowing orange magic into the barrier, perhaps to break it or drain it of its power.

They're trying to save me.

"Guys!" I shouted as I stumbled down the hill. "Stop!" When the tug of the Stryx pulled at me once more, I halted, gasping. Everyone turned to look at me. "Come on!"

Relief flashed on their faces. I didn't spare a second more. I just turned and ran, scrambling up the hillside. I had to get far, far away. The Stryx still had a hold on me, and I couldn't let them suck me back in. No way I could count on Hermes to save me twice.

I reached the top and began to slide down the hill on the other side, heading toward a low-lying bank of mist.

"Rowan! What's wrong?" Bree shouted from behind.

"Just need some"—I gasped, sprinting forward—"distance!"

I kept running, finally stumbling to a halt about halfway down. The sound of explosions was fainter here, and if my friends saw me start to zombie-walk back toward the Stryx, they'd stop me.

Panting, I dropped to my knees, trying to catch my breath. In the distance, the mist cleared a bit. I squinted toward it. Were there buildings there?

Yes, there were.

A small village sat in the valley between two hills, ancient and stalwart through the ages.

The village that will be destroyed by the Stryx if they keep going with this mad plan.

An ache started up in my chest. The buildings were small, little white houses of the style that were so recognizably Greek. A street led into the village, passing between two houses. I caught sight of a boy, no older than six. He stared at me with big dark eyes, his right arm wrapped around a big goofy dog.

The ache turned to a lightning bolt of fear.

That little boy would die if the explosions went on much longer. At best, he'd evacuate and lose his home. Lose everything. Even now, rubble from the overflow was spilling down the hillside toward them. It would bury the village soon enough.

My gaze went from the boy to the dog.

Fates, I have to fix this.

Panting, I stood and turned to watch Maximus, Bree, Ana, and Jude race down the mountain toward me, confusion and worry on their faces.

"What the heck is going on?" Ana demanded.

Maximus strode up to me and gripped my arms, concern on his handsome face. "What's wrong? Are you okay?"

I nodded, reaching up to clasp his hand with my own. Warmth flowed through me at the touch, and I smiled. "I'm fine. For now. But I can't get near those explosions. Not right now."

"Fates, you had me worried." He pulled me to him in a tight hug, and I squeezed him back. Warmth, comfort, acceptance. His touch made all of those flow through me, and I drank them up.

Finally, I pulled back and stepped away. Jude was nearly to us. I didn't think my teacher and hopefully future boss knew about us, and I wasn't sure what she would say. Not that her opinion would sway my feelings, but I didn't need any extra complications right now. I turned from Maximus to decrease suspicion, and looked at my sisters.

"What's the deal?" Bree reached out and grabbed my arm, as if wanting to assure herself that I was safe and alive.

"The Stryx dragged me to them." I shuddered at the memory of the loss of control. "I don't know how they managed it, but they're strong."

"You're the only one who could cross the barrier," Jude said.

"They protected their operations with a spell, and we can't get any closer. How did you get out?"

"Hermes, the Greek messenger god, saved me." I told them about the Amazons sending him and wanting to meet me. How I might be able to fix my power there, and I might even be able to get answers about what the Stryx were doing.

"Then you need to go," Jude said. "Without question."

"Yes." Bree's gaze was intense. "Anything that will help you get your magic under control."

I nodded. "I'll go."

"We'll stay here and try to find a way to break past their barriers and stop whatever they are doing." Jude's face paled. "Though you should hurry, Rowan. I don't know that we have anything in our arsenal that will work, and if they keep going, the village will be destroyed."

I had a horrible feeling that the village would be a relatively minor casualty of what the Stryx were planning. Something far worse would happen if they succeeded in their goals.

"I'll go with you," Maximus said.

My gaze flashed to him. "You will?"

"Why?" Jude asked, a glint in her eye.

Oh yeah, she was onto the fact that there was something between us. Hopefully I wouldn't get a talking-to about professionalism, given that he was my trainer. I'd have a hard time sitting through that and not saying something I shouldn't.

"The Order needs answers as much as you do," Maximus said. "And my colleagues can help you try to find a way to break through the Stryx's barrier. That's not my specialty. But I could help Rowan. And I want to." He turned to me. "I don't want you going alone into the unknown."

My eyes flared wide briefly. We'd shared a kiss and some serious sexual tension, but this was practically a proclamation that he cared for me.

And he'd said it in front of other people.

I nodded, trying to keep my face set in professional lines. "I could use some help, and since Bree and Ana will be busy here..." I trailed off, making it a question.

Jude nodded. "They will be."

"Then Maximus is definitely the perfect person," I said. "We work well together."

He nodded.

"Fine," Jude said. "I like the idea of you having backup. And if today in class was any indication, you need to take every opportunity you can get to learn to harness your magic."

Her words triggered a memory of Hermes's words. *Before the magic devours you.*

I swallowed hard and nodded, determined to fix my magic— and stop the Stryx—before *either* of them had a chance to devour me.

Jude looked at Bree and Ana. "Let's get back to it."

I hugged my sisters hard, whispering, "Be careful."

"You too." Bree squeezed my arms. "I know you can do this."

"No doubt in my mind," added Ana.

I smiled at them, blinking away the prick of tears and wondering why I was suddenly a bit weepy.

They hurried up the hill, and I turned to Maximus, holding up the transportation charm. "Can we stop by the Protectorate to grab some potion bombs? Do you have a transport charm?"

Maximus frowned. "You have your lightning and water magic now. And the death magic. Do you really need them?"

I could hear what was unspoken. He thought the potion bombs were my crutch. And maybe they were.

Still, I wanted them.

I raised the special transportation charm Hermes had given me.

"Wait a moment." He strode toward me and gently gripped

my arms. At his touch, I realized I hadn't been alone with him in days. He gazed down at me, a crease of concern between his brows. His blue eyes were intense. Too intense to look away. "Are you all right?"

"I'm fine."

"Really?"

"If I'm not, I'll be fine as soon as I figure out my magic."

A wry smile quirked up at the edge of his mouth. "You don't let anything get you down, do you?"

"I did once." I'd been down the whole time I was held by the Rebel Gods. I didn't want to end up like that again. "Keep on keepin' on, right?"

"It's not the worst motto in the world." He bent down and pressed a kiss to my forehead.

I leaned into him, reveling in his touch. But it wasn't enough.

I tilted my head back and pressed my lips to his, stealing a kiss. Not from him, since he gave it willingly. But from time, because it seemed we never had enough. His scent and taste wrapped around me, momentarily making me breathless.

The sound of an explosion tore through the quiet, making my insides vibrate.

I pulled back, slightly breathless. "We have more important things to be doing."

Maximus's gaze was hot as it met mine. "The only thing more important than kissing you is the end of the world."

I hiked a thumb over my shoulder. "Isn't that what this is?"

He nodded, his expression dire. "Indeed."

I stepped back and raised the transport stone.

"Do you know where we're going?" he asked.

"Istanbul. He said this would take me to the Amazons." I hurled the stone to the ground.

A glittery gold cloud burst forth. Not the usual silvery gray of a transport charm, so it must have been something special.

The ether sucked me in and spun me through space, then spit me out in the middle of a heaving, bustling city. Maximus appeared next to me, an anchor in a surging storm of people. I grabbed his arm as hundreds rushed by, all dressed in business suits.

Mid-morning rush?

I glanced up at Maximus. "Let's get out of here."

We pushed our way to the edge of the crowd, which was flowing down the sidewalk in one long stream of people. We tucked ourselves into a doorway nook that led into a shop, and I surveyed the crowd.

Where the heck were we?

A scan of the city street showed tall glass buildings piercing the blue sky, imposing sentinels of businesses that could be located anywhere in the world.

I had expected the Amazons to be ancient warrior women, living in some remote place and wearing old-school armor. Not these Amazons, though.

"I guess this is the closest big city to the shore of the Black Sea where they used to live." Given that most of my knowledge of the Amazons came from comics and Hermes, I was going to really need to bone up. "But where the hell do they live now?"

The place was huge, with millions of people, seemingly everywhere I looked.

"Hermes didn't give you directions?"

"He just said to look for a symbol of a warrior woman." My gaze snagged on a massively tall building. Right in the middle was a huge crest—a woman holding two swords crossed over her head. I pointed. "And *that* is pretty obvious."

I pushed my way through the crowd, moving quickly toward the building that looked like it was a center of international finance or something equally boring.

Seriously, what the hell were the Amazons doing here?

Maximus kept pace behind me since the crowd was flowing too thick and strong for us to walk side by side. When we finally spilled out into the stone courtyard in front of the building, I sucked in air, grateful for the space.

Huge glass doors beckoned, each of them two stories tall and etched with an image of ancient warrior women.

"Not subtle, are they?" I asked.

"I wouldn't be, if I were them," Maximus said. "And even if they're trying to blend with humans, no one would guess they're the real thing."

I stepped into the echoing foyer of the building. It was huge, seeming to take up the whole bottom floor, and nearly empty. The floor was a gleaming lake of black marble that shined under the modern steel chandeliers. A big granite desk occupied the middle of the space, and two women sat behind it, contemplating a chessboard between them.

As soon as my foot hit the marble floor on the interior side of the doorway, they stood, quickly going to attention, their gazes fixed on me and Maximus.

Well, they certainly weren't dressed like secretaries. Instead of skirts and blouses, they wore black tactical gear. Each wore a strange golden crystal around her neck.

Their stance was casually deadly, shoulders relaxed but hands close to the daggers sheathed at their thighs. It was hard to determine either woman's age, but there was something ancient about them. Powerful. The warriors might look like they were in their twenties, but they sure didn't feel like it.

I began to approach, closing the twenty-yard distance between us with Maximus at my side. My skin prickled with awareness. Familiarity, almost. The women raked their gazes up and down my form, clearly forming their first opinions about me.

Both were over six feet tall. The one on the left had straight dark hair and even features. Her brow was set in a firm line over dark eyes that missed no details. The one on the right wore her red hair up in a high ponytail that trailed down her back. Her face was softer, with rounded cheeks and fuller lips. But no one would mistake her for the weaker one. No one would mistake *either* of them for weak.

Real-life Amazons.

"How can we help you?" The redhead had a deeper voice than I'd expected, but it wasn't unfriendly.

"I'm, ah—looking for the Amazons. Hermes sent me."

Their brows flew up, and they glanced at each other. When they looked back at me, interest gleamed in their eyes.

"The new girl?" the brunette asked.

"Maybe?" I honestly had no idea.

The brunette's hand went for the dagger at her thigh. Quickly, she drew it from the sheath. As the metal slipped free of the leather, it grew and lengthened into a wickedly long sword.

Nice. The inane thought cut through my shock.

She lunged, and there was no more time for shock. Her sword swiped out for my neck, and very briefly, my life flashed before my eyes.

CHAPTER FIVE

As the dark-haired Amazon went for me, the redhead went for Maximus.

My attacker was fast, her blade zipping toward my neck. At the last moment, I ducked, going low to avoid her blade. The steel whistled overhead, so close that it might have severed a few hairs.

Heart pounding, I lunged away, catching sight of the redhead and Maximus fighting fast and hard.

Dang. This is not what I expected.

I reached into the ether and drew a sword, spinning to face the brunette who had followed me. She was fast and strong, swinging her blade like a pro as she bore down on me.

I dodged the steel once, twice, then got in a strike of my own, forcing her to dodge backward. I pressed my advantage, lunging with another swipe. This one made her duck, and I swung again, determined not to lose my lead.

But what should I do with it?

I didn't want to kill them. I needed to be here. I could feel it. These were my people, and information was within these tall glass walls. But if I didn't decide soon, I'd lose this advantage. The Amazon and I were too evenly matched.

Beside me, Maximus fought the other Amazon. She was strong and fast, but he had the advantage of height and strength. Their steel clashed as they parried, each taking the lead in turns.

I looked back at the dark-haired Amazon, since she was the one with the power to take off my head. I lunged for her again, but she grinned and leapt backward, lowering her sword.

I was still in strike mode and was barely able to pull back in time. I stopped right before my steel cut into her arm.

She grinned as if she'd known I'd stop. "Not bad."

The redhead darted away from Maximus, clearly taking a cue from her colleague that the fight was over. "Her man isn't bad, either."

My mouth opened. I almost said that he wasn't my man.

But then, was that even true? And I *wanted* him to be, if I were honest about it. Either way, that wasn't what I'd come here to discuss.

"What the hell is going on?" I asked.

"Just seeing if you measure up." The brunette stepped forward and stuck out her hand. "I'm Antimache."

I shook her hand, appreciating her strong grip but confused all the same. "Rowan. This is Maximus."

He just nodded his greeting, his eyes wary.

The redhead thrust her hand out. "I'm Melousa. We're glad you're here."

I shook her hand, my gaze taking in the entire space. "Were you expecting me?"

"Hoping," Antimache said.

"What is this place?" I asked.

Maximus was being oddly silent, but I appreciated it. This was kind of my show, and he wasn't the sort of man to need to be loud to make his presence known.

Melousa gestured for us to follow her. "Come, we'll introduce you to the queens."

"Queens? Plural?" Hermes had given two names, but I hadn't focused on it at the time. I followed them across the gleaming stone floor toward a bank of elevators on the far wall.

"Yes, plural," Melousa said. "Cooperation and teamwork have kept us alive this long. No point in stopping now."

I couldn't argue with that. It was how my sisters and I lived. Stronger together than apart.

The elevator dinged as the doors opened, and we stepped inside. The far wall was made of glass that looked out onto the street. A harried businessman walked by, his tie flapping in the wind as he shouted into a cell phone. It was a strangely human, normal scene, considering that I was standing with the ancient Amazons.

"Why did you move to a human city?" I asked.

"It was closest to our homeland by the Black Sea," Melousa said. "And it was time to get away from the countryside. We're not like some of the ancients, clinging to the past. We've moved into the modern world."

As the elevator zipped upward, revealing an amazing view of the city below, I couldn't help but agree. The Amazons had adapted, and they'd adapted *well*.

In the distance, I caught sight of a massive body of water. The Black Sea that she'd mentioned? I really needed to brush up on my geography. I glanced at Maximus, who looked impressed but wary.

Yep, just about how I feel.

The elevator doors dinged, and I turned as they opened, revealing a massive office where every wall was made of glass. There were two large desks in the room, as well as furniture and one of those archery targets. The whole place was decorated with a modern flair, everything showing sleek, simple lines. Except for a few ornate statues that looked to be thousands of years old. Definitely originals, heirlooms of their past.

No matter how far they'd moved into the future, they couldn't let go of what had come before.

I couldn't blame them. Neither could I.

Two women stood in the middle of the room, staring at the elevator doors as if they'd expected us.

Magic fairly rolled off of them, smelling like a fresh sea wind and sounding like battle—the clash of metal, the sound of footsteps pounding on the battle field, the cry of the fallen. It felt like the cut of a blade and tasted slightly metallic.

Whew. I would *not* want to mess with these ladies.

They were taller than the guards, a few inches over six feet, and they were dressed in a similar tactical gear with identical golden crystals around their necks. Dark and practical, an outfit made for war. They looked to be in their mid-forties, each with a long mane of dark hair and clever eyes that seemed to see right into my soul.

Without question, these were the queens.

On instinct, I bowed.

Maximus followed, his gaze assessing.

The one on the right stepped forward. "Finally, you are here."

I just nodded, not quite sure what to say.

"I am Queen Hippolyta," she said.

"And I am Queen Penthesilea."

Both of them had strong voices that echoed with command. They'd been queens for thousands of years, so I supposed it made sense.

"I'm Rowan Blackthorn, and this is Maximus Valerius. Why did you call me here?"

"You're one of us," Queen Hippolyta said. "We knew to expect you, but not quite when. Then you began inheriting your powers, and our seer could find your magical signature."

So it *was* timed with me becoming a DragonGod. Made sense.

"You're the only one of us born in the modern day." Queen Penthesilea walked toward me and pressed her hand to the side of my arm, as if she wanted to test that I was real. "Original, unique."

"It's been thousands of years since one of us was born," Queen Hippolyta said.

"But why me?"

Both queens shrugged.

"You must be worthy," Penthesilea said.

"I hope so," I said.

"It won't be easy." Queen Hippolyta's eyes turned serious. "Your magic is not resting easily inside you. The powers of the gods are not settling in well because you have too much. And you are missing the power that the Rebel Gods took from you."

"I can't change that." The words snapped out of me as the memory of the stone sitting in my apartment flared in my mind. That stone contained the magic the Rebel Gods had stolen from me. My sisters had gotten the magic back for me and stored it in a hunk of rock. It was the only place it could stay now. Useless. "It's tainted with their darkness. I don't want that inside me."

I already had enough. I might not know how to get rid of the darkness the Rebel Gods had left within my soul, but I'd shoved it so far down inside me that it couldn't come to the surface anymore. No way I'd add anything to it. That might upset the balance within me, turning me forever toward the dark.

No way.

"We know," Queen Penthesilea said. "That magic is too dark.

Without all of your birth magic, it will make it harder for you to learn to harness the magic of the gods, but you will manage."

"You must," Queen Hippolyta said.

I nodded. "But how?"

"Prove yourself. Help us."

"Help you with what? What do you do, exactly?" From the look of their office, they were businesswomen. Yet they were dressed for war.

"We run Amazonian Security and Defense," Queen Hippolyta said. "We've decided to use our powers for good. After living for so long, seeing the suffering in the world, we decided to leave our settlement and help."

"But you're in an office building?" I asked. It seemed like such a weird place.

"Come, you'll see." Queen Penthesilea gestured for us to follow her to the elevator, and I did.

At some point, the guards who'd greeted us had disappeared, silently melting away. I shot Maximus a look, but couldn't read his expression.

This was a bit like meeting his in-laws, though we weren't really that far along in our relationship. But this was where I had come from, in a way.

Anxiety made my blood race as I stepped into a different elevator than before. There were two on the same wall.

Honestly, I was nervous about what I would find.

Probably wouldn't matter, actually. I didn't have much choice. I was an Amazon, and if I didn't get my act together, my magic would devour me.

No magic. No soul. Simple as that.

This elevator contained glass doors instead of a glass wall so we could see into the building rather than out. At first, we passed by a few boring floors showing nothing but hallways.

When we reached the first massive, hollowed-out section of the skyscraper, I gaped.

It was a war room. Or a training room, at least. It had to be an area about six stories high. The ceiling loomed overhead. Women stood along one wall, firing arrows toward the targets on the other side.

"You can see that we've modified the space," Queen Hippolyta said.

"You sure have."

The elevator descended to another large, open space. This one was even taller. Twelve stories, perhaps. There were balconies lining the exterior of the walls, and women jumped off them, attached to ropes as they fired their weapons while they fell. Beyond them, the glass walls revealed the city in the distance.

It took everything I had to keep my jaw from dropping.

"The windows are tinted, of course," Queen Hippolyta said. "The humans don't know quite what we do here, though we often fight on their behalf."

"They don't know that, either," Queen Penthesilea said.

"What do you do for them?" I asked.

"Turn the tides of petty wars, primarily," Queen Hippolyta said. "In remote places where our interference can go unnoticed."

"Impressive." Maximus's brow was set, and it was hard to figure out exactly what he was thinking. But he clearly liked what he saw, from the tone of his voice. It looked a bit like the Colosseum, really, a massive arena where warriors fought. But here, they fought because they wanted to. They fought for a cause they believed in.

I could get behind that.

The elevator stopped at the next large, open space. A few Amazons were practicing hand-to-hand in the middle of the room, their moves so fast and their technique so skilled that I couldn't help but be impressed.

I wanted to train with them. I could learn so much here.

The doors dinged and opened. Queen Hippolyta stepped forward. "We'll stop here. There are more levels, but you get the point."

"Yeah, you're good at what you do," I said.

"Very." Queen Penthesilea's voice lacked any modesty, and I liked it. The modesty would sound weird anyway. She was an ancient queen who oversaw a massive, modern-day team of warriors who worked to save the world.

Badass.

Maximus and I followed them to a collection of firm-looking couches. We sat, facing the warriors who fought on the mats in the middle of the room.

"What role do I play in this?" I asked.

"First, you must prove yourself worthy," Queen Penthesilea said. "As all great heroes do."

I liked the sound of that.

Who wouldn't?

A hero.

I'd stood in my sisters' shadow—a shadow they rightfully cast, and I was proud as hell of them—but I wouldn't mind stepping out of it. Joining them.

"What do I need to do? Fight a monster?" Heracles had fought a ton of monsters. Jason too. All the Greek heroes had.

A wry smile tugged at the corner of Queen Hippolyta's mouth. "You already are."

"The Stryx." Of course it was the Stryx. They were my trial.

"Precisely."

"That's one reason I'm here," I said. "Not just because you called and I need answers about what I am. But because the

Stryx are blowing holes in the earth near a village. They're going to destroy it."

"That's not all the damage they'll do." Queen Penthesilea shook her head. "And no, before you ask, I don't know what they are after. Only that they have been a great evil, since long before you were born. They lay dormant for millennia, but they have risen now. Whatever they want, it is not good for anyone except them."

"And I have to stop them."

"Yes, but first you must fix the magic inside you." Queen Hippolyta's face turned serious. I'd thought it was serious before, but the lines that now creased the sides of her mouth and the heaviness in her green eyes made it clear that *something* was about to be said that I might not like. "But first, we need your help."

My brow wrinkled in confusion. "What do you mean?"

Queen Hippolyta reached for the crystal that hung around her neck. The one that I'd noticed earlier. She removed it, and the air shimmered around her.

Suddenly, she didn't look quite so strong and whole anymore. Her muscles seemed to deflate in front of my eyes, her neck turning skinny and her collarbones jutting out way too far. Her cheekbones became prominent and her eyes sank into their hollows. Even her hair looked lank and dull.

Queen Penthesilea removed her necklace as well, undergoing the same transformation, aging before my eyes.

I stifled a gasp. No way in hell I'd want people gasping at me if I were in their shoes, so I kept my yap shut. "What's wrong?"

I got the words out in a mostly normal tone of voice, but my insides trembled. These women were so powerful, so strong. They did so much good in the world and held the answers to what I was.

But they were dying.

No question about it. The crystal contained a glamour that hid the truth. And I did *not* like the truth. Grief twisted through me at the idea of their loss. An ancient race dedicated to protecting others, and they might all be wiped out.

"Whatever is happening with the Stryx is making us ill," Queen Hippolyta said.

"We *think*," Queen Penthesilea said.

Queen Hippolyta shot her a wry look. "My sister has always been the skeptic. But this began just recently. *Very recently.* About the time that the Stryx began carving into the earth. Whatever it is progresses quickly. We think it is related to the Stryx. So does our most powerful seer."

"How can I help? Is it affecting all of the Amazons?"

"All of them except you," Queen Penthesilea said. "We believe you are protected by the strength of your magic."

"We need a cure, but we don't know how to find one and we're too weak to try," Queen Hippolyta said. "There's only one person who might know. Atlas."

The name rang a bell. "The guy who holds up the world?"

"The titan," Queen Penthesilea said. "Many thousands of years ago, when the titans and the gods warred, the titans lost. Atlas and Prometheus were the only titans not thrown into Tartarus."

"Prometheus was chained up so that an eagle could eat his liver over and over again, right? And Atlas was asked to hold up the world."

"The celestial heavens, actually," Queen Hippolyta said. "Though his role has changed. Same for Prometheus. He got away from the eagle long ago, but he's still a bit of a disaster from what I hear."

Queen Penthesilea leaned forward. "Atlas helps keep the magic in the heavens from interfering with satellites. His role is vital."

"We need help with that sort of thing?" Maximus asked.

"Just a bit," she said. "Human progress usually moves forward without magic interfering. They exist in harmony most of the time. But when humans began sending satellites to space, they interacted negatively with the magic in the heavens. So Atlas stepped in. He used to hold up the celestial heavens; now he holds up the satellites. So to speak."

"But he's sick," Queen Hippolyta said. "He tried to get a message to us, but it was garbled. It's clear that he is deathly ill, like us. He's retreated. Or he's trapped. We don't know."

"How are you linked to Atlas?" Maximus asked. "Are all members of the Greek pantheon ill?"

"Hermes looked okay," I said.

"We don't think everyone is ill," Queen Penthesilea said. "All of the Amazons are, and Atlas and Prometheus. But the gods are fine. Other mythical creatures as well. But we've been linked to Atlas for thousands of years. Humans know that we were the enemies of the Greek gods. Most of the time, at least. What many do not realize is that we fought on the side of the titans in their war against the gods. We should have been thrown into Tartarus with them when the war ended, but Atlas saved us. He smuggled us away by giving us a bit of his magic. We've been linked ever since. We're not close to him anymore—it's been thousands of years—so we don't know where he is. But the ties that bind us are still there."

"So if he's sick and you're sick, it's the same thing," Maximus said.

"We believe so," Queen Hippolyta said. "It's magic, not true illness. And Atlas is the only one who might have an answer. Our seer prophesied that you can help us."

"We're too weak to leave, anyway." Queen Penthesilea gave a sad laugh. "Thousands of years of being the strongest, and now we are laid low."

"Not for long." I leaned forward and gripped her hand. "I will fix this."

I had no idea how, but I wasn't going to let my new family suffer like this. Another thought popped into my head. *Oh, shit.* "If Atlas dies from this, what happens to the satellites?"

"They fail," Queen Hippolyta said. "The magic that is so strong in outer space will eat away at them quickly."

Shit. A world without satellites would be chaos.

"And if they fail, it would be catastrophic," Queen Penthesilea said. "Human militaries rely heavily on satellites. Our seer has prophesied that if all of their communications go out, one of the great militaries will interpret it as an act of war by a foreign power. A massive world war will break out as a result."

My stomach dropped. "World War III?"

"Precisely." Queen Hippolyta's skin was pale at the thought.

So I wasn't just saving the Amazons. I was saving *everyone*.

"Do you have any idea where I should start?" I had no idea how to find a titan.

"With Prometheus, the only other titan who is not locked up in Tartarus," Queen Penthesilea said. "Atlas tried to get us a message, so he may have tried with Prometheus as well. Perhaps Prometheus knows more. We've heard he is in Istanbul. Apparently he likes to spend time at the Bosphorus bar. You may be able to find him there. He likes his drink."

So would I, if I had memories of my liver being eaten out of me by an eagle, over and over again.

"He's a wary bastard," Queen Hippolyta said. "Always on edge, thinking he'll be captured. I suggest that only one of you approach him. Keep his suspicions at bay."

I nodded. We could do that.

Queen Penthesilea reached into her pocket and handed me an elegant business card. "If you need anything—weapons, transportation, knowledge—call us."

My hand closed around the card.

"And be careful," Queen Hippolyta said. "He hates our kind."

"So he could hate me." *Great.*

Queen Hippolyta smiled. "Just don't let him know what you are."

CHAPTER SIX

The Bosphorus bar was a little hole in the wall, far from the business district. Here, the buildings were older, smaller. The crowd was different too. Fewer slick business suits and people yelling into their cell phones.

As we approached the bar, Maximus reached for my hand. "Be careful. I'll have my eye on you."

I squeezed his hand. "Thanks. Back atcha."

"I'll enter a few minutes after you and stick near the bar. If you need me, make a signal."

I grinned. "It'll probably be real obvious." I doubted that there'd be a subtle, *save me from this awkward conversation* gesture. More like a knockdown, drag-out fight. "You won't miss it."

Though hopefully we could avoid it. All I needed was info on how to find Atlas, and I needed it fast. No fight necessary.

Near the door, I let go of Maximus's hand. I wanted to lean up and press a kiss to his cheek, but I'd probably better not. I needed to be on my game, not on him.

"Be careful." His soft words followed me toward the door.

I pushed it open and stepped inside the dimly lit interior.

The bar was small and narrow against the left wall, with little tables crowding the rest of the space. Prometheus's magic hit me in the chest as soon as I entered, and I nearly stumbled.

It smelled of fire and tasted of peaches, followed by the sensation of heat and the sound of an eagle screeching.

Man, titans were powerful.

This had to be an all-supernatural bar if he was letting his signature hang out like that. If he was so obsessed with hiding, why was he making such a big show of it?

Idiot.

I scanned the bar, spotting him easily. He sat in the back corner, a big man hunched over a little table. His eyes were slightly bleary and his face haggard. Clothes rumpled and shoes untied.

Ah, yep.

Drunk.

So that explained the over-the-top magical signature.

Jeez, poor guy.

Honestly, the Greek gods were bastards as far as I could tell. All Prometheus had done was give the humans fire. That hardly deserved eternal torment. He'd escaped, clearly, but the torture had left its mark.

I approached his table, debating my first words.

I didn't get a chance to utter them.

"Who are you?" His voice was surly as I stopped in front of his table. He actually wasn't a bad-looking guy, just rough around the edges.

"I'm Rowan."

"*What* are you?"

Um...

He held up a finger. "Wait, wait. I've got it." He pointed at me. "You're a...DragonGod."

I frowned at him. "How could you tell?"

It wasn't something that was obvious at first glance, I was sure of it.

He shrugged. "Titan. I know stuff."

I sank into the seat across from him, noting the strange, empty glass on the table. It was shaped roughly like a test tube, with a residual milky liquid clinging to the inside of the glass. "That's what I'm here to talk to you about."

"Like what?" He scratched his sandy blond hair, his expression making it clear that the wheels were turning very creakily inside his head.

Yeah, Prometheus had been through some stuff, all right.

"Yeah." I nodded. "I need to know where Atlas is."

He scowled. "Why would I tell you that?"

"Well, I was hoping—"

"Another?" A feminine voice sounded from over my shoulder, and I turned.

A tall, dark-haired woman stood there, tray propped on her hip. Her brows were darkly lined and her lipstick red as she smacked away at some gum.

"Several," Prometheus slurred.

The woman's gaze landed on me. "And you?"

"Coffee, please."

"They're for her." Prometheus pointed to me. "And several for me too."

"How many is several?" She arched a dark brow.

"You choose, honey."

She turned and left, a bored expression on her face.

I looked at Prometheus. "I'm not here to drink."

"Well, you're not here to get information, either. Because I'm"—he stabbed a finger at his chest—"not talking."

"Are you sure about that?"

As he pondered the question for a little too long, I felt the air change in the room. The door slammed shut.

Maximus must have entered. I could feel the weight of his gaze, just briefly.

I turned slightly, my gaze landing on him. He was headed to the bar, no longer looking at me. Dang, he looked good in here. Tall and fit and towering over the little tables.

I turned back to Prometheus. "It's sure taking a while for you to decide."

"Decide what?"

Yeah, this dude was drunk. And maybe if I could get him a little drunker, he'd get chatty.

The waitress appeared a moment later, six test tubes of clear liquid on her tray. A pitcher of water accompanied them. She offloaded her cargo. "Call if you want anything."

"We will, sweetie."

Ugh, Prometheus. With the "sweeties" and "honeys." He might look like a young man, but he sounded like an old one.

"Do you like Raki?" he asked.

"No idea."

He poured a bit of water into each test tube, and the liquid turned a milky white. "Traditional Turkish drink. Will burn the lining right off your throat."

"Sounds tasty."

He shrugged. "Can be."

He raised the glass to his mouth, and I followed suit, chugging back the white liquid. It burned like fire going down, and I coughed.

"It's *not* tasty," I sputtered.

Prometheus smacked his lips. "You might change your mind."

I wasn't so sure about that. Give me a nice beer any day.

"Another!" Prometheus poured the water into the next two glasses, and we drank.

As I swallowed the burning stuff—thankfully keeping my

coughing to a minimum this time—my fingertips found the little vial of potion in my belt that I was definitely going to need. Sober Up tonic would be my saving grace tonight, because no way I could drink Prometheus under the table. This guy was a pro. I had a feeling that being a titan helped.

As we drank the third glass of Raki, I felt Maximus's gaze drilling into me. Probably worried about my alcohol consumption. Couldn't blame him. I was knocking them back.

Throat on fire, I set down my glass and leaned toward Prometheus. "So, tell me about Atlas."

"Why do you want to know about that loser?"

"He's sick, and I need to help him." In fact, Prometheus didn't look so good himself, now that I was up close and really looking. I'd thought his rough look was from the alcohol, and maybe it was, but he also had the wasted muscles and prominent collarbones that the Amazons had had. He wasn't as bad off, but I'd bet he was sick, too.

"He doesn't need your help. He's doing fine." He frowned. "Though he did send that message. Couldn't understand anything in it. But he's probably fine."

"I don't think he is. I don't think you are, either." Whatever the cure was for this disease, I was going to have to make a batch for him. "I'll help you if you'll help me."

"I'll help you if you have another drink." He gave me a lecherous leer.

"Oh, come on, dude. Don't be creepy."

He huffed and sat back.

"I'm not getting in the sack with you, even if you get me totally drunk."

"Well, I'm not telling you anything about Atlas."

Actually, he'd already been a little loose-lipped. My plan was a good one. "Let's drink to it."

He grinned and waved at the waitress. A few minutes later,

she appeared with six more test tubes of Raki.

Ah, shit.

That was a lot of liquor. I liked the occasional beer every now and again, but this?

This was nuts.

But when Prometheus poured the water into the glass to turn it a milky white, I picked it up and slugged it back. I was definitely going to have to take some Sober Up soon.

"Nice to have a drinking buddy," Prometheus slurred. "But I think you could use a word of advice."

"Yeah?" My head was already woozy.

"Yeah. You're a DragonGod, so you gotta act like one."

I squinted at him. "What the heck is that supposed to mean?

"Don't fight the magic. Embrace it."

"But it could devour me." I shivered. "And there's darkness inside me."

Yep, I was a bit more drunk than I'd realized.

"There's darkness in everyone, kid. And the magic will devour you if you fight it."

"Am not."

"Are too." He handed me another glass, and I slugged it back. My head spun a bit. "Do you mean I have to embrace the dark magic inside me?"

"I mean you have to stop hiding. Embrace your destiny—embrace *all* your magic. Even the stuff you're scared of."

I didn't want to face the stuff I was scared of—that was the whole point of being scared of it. To then do some serious avoiding. But if all of these gods were going to give me some of their power, I had to do something to be worthy of it. And facing my fears seemed like part of that.

Maybe this was how I was meant to learn about myself and my magic. Just randomly, from drunken titans.

Not what I'd expected, but hey, what did I know?

Prometheus pushed the last glass of milky white liquid toward me and raised a brow.

I tossed it back, delighted to see him sway slightly to the right. Good. He was feeling it, too.

And I needed to *not* be feeling it. I stood. "Be right back."

He just grunted. I wasn't worried he'd leave while I was gone. Prometheus looked like he planned to have his butt nailed to that chair for a while yet. Not to mention, he probably couldn't walk. Not with all the Raki in his system. How much had he had before I'd gotten here?

I wobbled my way between the little tables, heading for a darkened back hallway that I assumed led to the ladies' room. Maximus was no longer at the bar, and a little stab of sadness hit me. Where had he gone?

The darkened hallway led to a tiny bathroom, where I multi-tasked by peeing and taking my Sober Up potion at the same time. Never say a girl doesn't have skills.

My head began to clear immediately, but even Sober Up couldn't fight six Rakis. I had to guess that I was down to two in my system now—mildly drunk. I definitely had enough wits about me to stay on top of Prometheus, though.

I opened the door.

A looming figure blocked the way. I bit back a scream and sent my fist flying, drunk instinct driving me.

The figure caught my fist. "Didn't mean to scare you."

Maximus. My vision had adjusted enough that I could see him in the slight light of the hallway, his features cast in shadow. He looked so much like a fallen angel that I wanted to peek at his back and see if he had wings.

I knew he didn't, though, because there was just a little bit of the devil inside him.

I leaned back to look up at him. "You scared the hell out of me."

"Are you doing all right out there? You're drinking like a fish."

"I'm fine. I had some Sober Up, and now I'm only 20 percent drunk."

"That's not bad, but it's not ideal."

"It is when I'm trying to drink information out of our titan buddy."

"Ah, that's your plan."

"I don't think he'll give it up any other way." Boy, did Maximus smell good. Like cedar and the ocean. I leaned closer, trying to get a better whiff, then realized I looked insane. I pulled back. "Better get in there again. I think I've almost got him."

"Good luck. I've got your back."

He could have my anything-he-wanted.

When I reached the table where Prometheus still sat, propped up by some kind of magic or determination or just sheer drunk luck, there were six more test tubes on the table.

"Well, shit," I muttered.

"If you're going to try to drink me under the table, I'm going to win."

"We'll see about that." I sat heavily in my chair, convinced I'd be victorious. Because I was cheating. I still had another half dose of Sober Up, in case I needed it.

I stared blearily at the glass containers of clear liquid.

I was going to need it.

Quickly, Prometheus added a bit of water to the vials, performing the cool little chemistry experiment with turning the liquid white. I didn't know what was going on with it, but my curiosity to know more would probably die in the daylight when I opened my eyes to the inevitable hangover. Sober Up was no match for Prometheus and Raki.

I slugged back the three of them, making sure Prometheus

did the same, then leaned over the table to catch Prometheus's eye. "So, you live in Istanbul."

"Yep."

I asked him questions, nothing interesting, just getting him to talk about himself while the liquor went to work. When I slipped in a question about Atlas, he was so used to babbling that it slipped right out.

"If I were you, I'd check the Garden of Hesperides."

Jackpot. "Why?"

"Why, what?" He blinked, his eyes hazy.

"Why would I check the Garden of Hesperides?"

"Why the hell would you go there?"

Ah, crap. We were on a merry-go-round of drunk questions. And honestly, with the new dose of Raki coursing through my system, it wasn't helping matters. "I'd go there to find Atlas. Will I find him there?"

"No, but you'll find his daughters." He blinked at me, then scowled. "Hey, that was what you wanted to know."

"Huh? What are you talking about?" Yeah, that was what I wanted to know, but no reason to piss him off with my victory. Better to play drunk. It wasn't hard. I swayed slightly, putting on a show. "I wonder if there's anything dangerous in the Garden of Hesperides?"

"Oh yeah, loads of dangerous things," Prometheus slurred as he held up a hand and pointed to one finger, about to count things off a list. "There's the dragon, the—"

He swayed once more, then face-planted on the table.

Aw, crap.

I leaned forward and poked his shoulder. "Hey, Prometheus. Hey! You awake?"

He barely mumbled something. He was basically the equivalent of a godly rock.

Damn it.

Looked like that was all the info I was going to get out of him.

I turned to look for Maximus, who was sitting at the bar, staring at us with a frown. The dark-haired bartender was headed our way, her gaze on Prometheus. She didn't look annoyed though. Far from it.

"How's our big guy doing here?" she said.

"Um, not great? I think he passed out." I felt a bit guilty. Clearly Prometheus was an alcoholic. While I'd needed the info to save the world, I didn't want to add to his troubles.

Should have thought of that earlier, genius.

The waitress stopped by and rubbed his hair. He didn't move. "Ah, don't worry about old Prometheus here."

"I feel like I should. He seems like he needs help."

She scoffed. "Not him. He's on a job, apparently. Said he had to wait here and help some girl. Give her some information." Her gaze sharpened, and I realized that up until now, she'd looked a bit dimwitted. "Hey, could that girl have been you?"

Now it was my turn to feel a bit dimwitted. "Wait, what?"

"Did he help you?"

He had, in fact.

Hang on, had I just been played by Prometheus? Had he been waiting for *me*?

I'd definitely needed his help, and it was for an important cause. I had no idea how he'd known to expect me, but that was what seers were for. As for why he'd relayed the information in such a weird manner, I had no idea. Maybe he was just bored after thousands of years hanging around earth.

"Either way," the waitress said. "We'll watch out for him. Don't worry a bit. And he already paid the tab."

My gaze darted between her and him. "All right, then. Thanks."

I got up and hot-footed it out of there, though my hot-footing was a bit leaden from all the Raki. By the time I reached Maximus, my head was really spinning. He stood up from his stool at the bar and gripped my arm gently, keeping me upright.

"Did you get what you needed?" He peered down at me, concern glinting in his eyes.

"Yeah, let's get out of here." I swayed my way to the door, Maximus keeping me upright.

The night air was brisk when we stepped outside, the city lights gleaming all around. The high rises in the distance looked like an entirely separate universe from this small, older part of the city.

I leaned drunkenly into Maximus, burrowing my face into his jacket to get a whiff of his scent. My head spun as I tried to remember why we were here.

"What did you learn?" he asked.

The repeated question jogged my memory. "We're looking for the Garden of Hesperides. Atlas's daughters live there, and maybe they can tell us where he is. Oh, and there's something dangerous there. A...uh....a..." I scrubbed my hand over my face. "Damn it, I can't remember what the dangerous thing was."

"It's okay. I'm sure we'll figure it out." Maximus's deep voice drew my attention upward.

I looked at him, struck dumb by how freaking hot he was. He stood in the shadow of the streetlamp, his features carefully highlighted by their glow. Broad shoulders blocked the light from hitting my face, though, and I couldn't help but think of those shoulders looming over me in other circumstances as well.

"Wow, you're pretty," I slurred.

"Pretty?"

"Well, maybe not pretty." Drop-dead gorgeous, more like. Lethally sexy. Fallen angel broody hot.

I couldn't help myself. I leaned upward and pressed my lips to his. Heat and desire shot through me, straight to my core. It twisted, tying me in knots and making me desperate to latch myself onto him.

So I did, throwing my arms around him and kissing him for all I was worth. My tongue snuck inside his mouth, and he groaned low in his throat, sounding almost like an animal.

His strong arms reached around my back, pulling me toward him so that I was pressed against the full length of his hard chest. My head spun with desire and need.

We should have sex. Right now.

Like, right here.

He groaned again, then pulled back, separating his mouth from mine. "We can't do this right now."

I almost screeched my indignation, but my brain was moving way too slow to even get the noise out. Wait, why couldn't I speak?

Why could I barely move? I felt like I was existing in water, swimming almost.

Oh yeah, drunk as a skunk.

Maximus moved me back from him just slightly, carefully holding my arms to keep me upright. "You're a bit too drunk. Once you've sobered up a bit, we can revisit this." The corner of his mouth tugged up at one corner. "Hopefully you'll still think it's a good idea by then."

Oh, I will.

I wanted to say the words, but they wouldn't squeak out past my lips. Even worse, my stomach chose that moment to lurch.

Oh, hell.

Suddenly, my lethargic muscles got a shot of adrenaline, and I could move. I was filled with a sheer, animal panic induced by the horrifying vision of puking on my hot sorta-boyfriend's shoes.

I turned, jerking away from his grasp and leaning over to heave Raki up onto the sidewalk. Impossibly, it burned even more going in this direction, and I regretted my stupid plan to drink answers out of Prometheus.

When the last of the Raki seemed to have left the building, I stood, wobbly.

Concern creased Maximus's brow as he pulled a water bottle out of his pocket and handed it to me. "Here, I got this from the bar."

He held on to me as I stood shakily, drinking the water. It felt like actual heaven going down my throat, and I figured he was pretty much the biggest genius in the world to have remembered to grab the bottle.

"I thought you took the Sober Up," he said.

"I did. I just drank waaaay too much."

"Do you have any more?"

"Yeah," I slurred. Clearly, puking didn't really help the drunkenness. What was in my blood was already there. "Pink vial, in my belt."

His fingertips moved lightly over my potions belt, and he tugged out a little glass vial and held it up in front of my face. "This one?"

I nodded, my head feeling very bobbly, then drank the last of the potion. My mind cleared a bit, but I was still a lightweight. The alcohol wasn't entirely out of my system, but at least the Sober Up would prevent alcohol poisoning. I might have had nine drinks, but I had a feeling they counted for more than one alcohol unit each. Who knows how much I'd really had?

"Come on." Maximus wrapped an arm around my waist and tugged me along to walk beside him. "Let's find a place to stay the night so you can sleep this off."

"Faaaantastic idea." I stumbled, almost face-planting.

Maximus swept me up into his arms and strode down the street. He was so warm. So lovely. So...

Blackness took me.

CHAPTER SEVEN

A beam of sunlight dragged me from sleep. At first, I thought it was the devil himself, shining hellfire into my eyes. Then I realized it was just the morning sun, streaming through the windows and landing right. On. My. Face.

Groggily, I opened my eyes.

At first, I could see nothing.

Then there was just a broad expanse of male chest. I blinked, confused, and nearly lunged backward. Then I caught sight of Maximus's face, dead asleep.

Oh. Him.

Well, that I could get down with.

But what were we doing, naked in bed together? Wouldn't I remember something like that?

And what the hell was digging into my rib cage? Wincing, I peered down. Crap, it was my bra. Under my shirt.

Which meant there'd been no hanky-panky. That was actually a good thing, because if it was going to happen, I certainly wanted to remember it. I was *damned* sure I'd remember it with Maximus, even if it was bad. Mostly because I'd be so shocked it wasn't any good. So shocked I'd probably tell my grandkids about it. *Well, there was once this really hot guy,* I could imagine myself saying in a creaky voice.

Okay, maybe not. That wasn't quite PG-13.

But if he was naked and I was not, and I couldn't remember...

I must have been drunk.

I wasn't that hungover, thank fates, which was a miracle from the heavens. Hazy memories of a bar, glasses of white stuff, and a surly man filtered through my mind. Prometheus.

Okay, so I'd gotten some info out of him. That was good. Then Maximus must have dragged me back here, semi-conscious or possibly unconscious, and we'd slept it off.

Speaking of, where *was* here?

I craned my neck, careful not to bounce the bed and disturb Maximus, and caught sight of a nice hotel suite. There were two large beds, with three tiny figures curled up on the other bed.

The Menacing Menagerie. How had they gotten here? I didn't remember them showing up. At least they were asleep.

I turned back to Maximus, who looked so good in the morning light. The sharp planes of his features were relaxed in sleep, his full lips parted just slightly. His lashes were so damned long that I was jealous, but mostly I just wanted to lean up and kiss him.

I nearly did it, too. Then I caught a whiff of my own breath, and *holy crap.*

This time, I did lunge backward, desperate to get away and into the shower. I wasn't quite as graceful as I'd planned to be, and instead of sneakily sliding across the bed and making my escape, I crashed to the floor, dragging the bedsheets with me.

Well, hell.

"Are you okay?" Maximus's voice was thick with sleep.

Cheeks burning, I peeked up over the side of the bed. He wasn't, in fact, totally naked. It was almost worst. He wore some kind of tight black shorts that made my imagination run wild and my cheeks heat even more.

Since there was no chance of me gracefully rising to my feet and him forgetting what had happened, I considered just wrapping up in the sheet and rolling across the floor into the bathroom.

Maybe he wouldn't see me then.

Okay, nope, crap plan.

"Yeah, I'm fine." I struggled upright, the sheet wanting to keep me in a pile on the floor. "Going to grab a shower."

My whole body had to be red as I hurried into the bathroom. To his credit, Maximus didn't laugh. Or if he did, he did it quiet enough to keep my pride mostly intact. I appreciated that. A real solid dude, that one. Just acting like me on the floor in a pile of sheets was totally normal.

I showered as quickly as I could, washing away the mild effects of the hangover. Since I couldn't find my clothes and what I'd been wearing was definitely dirty, I put on the cushy hotel bathrobe and felt quite fancy. By the time I made it out into the suite, Maximus was dressed in a change of clothes that he'd probably conjured. The suite was much larger than I'd realized, with a little couch and table and a magnificent view of the city.

The table was covered in pretty much every breakfast food imaginable, along with a lot that I'd never even seen before. Maybe it was Turkish. My tongue tingled.

"Where did all this come from?" I drifted over as if I were in a trance, my stomach gurgling a waltz to accompany me.

"Room service is quick here."

"I bet, in a swanky place like this." My gaze moved over to the Menacing Menagerie, who all sat on the bed now, eyes riveted to the table. "You guys can share, you know."

Romeo waved his hand. *No, no. You go first.*

"No need to stand on ceremony."

No, really. If you eat first, then maybe mess the plates around some. It'll be more like trash.

Poppy and Eloise both nodded, their eyes bright with excitement. The little blue flower tucked behind Eloise's ear trembled.

Mess them up good. Romeo grinned, his white teeth gleaming.

"All right, then." They were weirdos, but they were *my* weirdos.

Maximus and I sat at the table, and my brain stalled temporarily at the sight of all the offerings. How in the world was I supposed to choose?

"Just eat some of everything," Maximus said, as if he'd read my mind. "That's what I plan to do."

"This is fantastic."

Maximus grinned up at me, his plate piled high. "I thought you'd like it." He shrugged. "So do I. Room service like this is one of the major perks of the modern era. Along with plumbing, the combustion engine, and vaccines."

"Pancakes are up there with vaccines?"

"What's the point of living if you don't have pancakes?" He grinned and took a bite of the aforementioned cake.

"You make a valid point, sir." I turned to my food, thinking about the hardship he had lived through. I forgot about it often, since he seemed like a normal modern man most of the time.

But just like Prometheus wasn't able to forget his terrible past with the eagle that perpetually ate his liver, Maximus would never forget his time in Ancient Rome. And I didn't need to ask to confirm that it wasn't the bad food or lack of electricity that he wanted to forget. It was the time in the Colosseum. His time as a slave whose job it was to murder.

But he'd escaped. He'd saved himself just like I would save myself. Like I would save the Amazons and the village and the whole world.

Because I didn't have any choice.

I turned my mind away from such heavy thoughts before performance anxiety froze me solid.

The banquet spread out before me deserved my full attention, and I was determined to enjoy the feast that looked like something out of a movie.

I tucked into the buffet, barely stopping myself from eating until I couldn't move. Between bites, I asked, "Did we get what we needed last night?"

"We did indeed, thanks to your quick talking."

"And quick drinking." I sipped some coffee that tasted like a dream. "Where are we headed?"

"The Garden of the Hesperides, to look for Atlas's daughters."

"Where's that?"

"Beats me. I think it's somewhere in Greece."

"I can ask the Amazons. They'll know." I pushed back from the table and looked at the Menacing Menagerie. "Did I mess it up enough?"

Romeo shrugged. *Not quite trash, but it still looks pretty tasty.*

He hopped over to the end of the bed near the table, and I ruffled his head. "I know you like to work for your food, but today you can have a bit of a lie-in."

The animals each took a chair and began to eat, really quite nicely. Eloise's table manners were exceptional, in fact. The badger looked like she could have tea with the queen. Except, of course, for the fact that she was a badger.

I rifled through my dirty clothes to find my cell phone and the card that Queen Hippolyta had given me, then dialed the number.

Within minutes, we had a plan. I hung up the phone and looked at Maximus. "We need to meet them on the roof."

"The roof?"

I grinned. "We're getting a ride."

~

When the helicopter landed on the roof twenty minutes later, I had to admit that I felt a bit like James Bond. It would have been faster to transport, but our charms were valuable. And without knowing exactly where the garden was, we might not have ended up in the right place. Once we were done, we should be able to transport out.

"Damn, this is cool." I grinned at Maximus.

He looked mildly green around the gills but nodded gamely.

The helicopter was sleek and black, and I'd have bet twenty bucks it had some kind of stealth equipment on it. The door slid open, and an Amazon leaned out, her blonde hair blowing in the wind.

She waved us forward, shouting, "Come on!"

I sprinted for the helicopter, ducking low under the whirling rotor even though I was pretty sure they were too high to take off my head. Better safe than sorry.

Wind whipped at my hair as I scrambled into the helicopter and buckled into one of the seats.

The pilot turned around, a big grin on her face. She looked about sixty, with brown hair to her shoulders and round dark sunglasses. "I'm Captain Neilson. We'll have you there in a flash!"

Maximus settled in next to me, and the helicopter took off, the roar of the rotor blasting my ears as the city fell away below.

The Amazon who sat in the seat across from us grinned, tossing us some headsets. I put mine on, and the world went a little quieter.

Her voice filtered through the earpieces. "We'll be there in about an hour. This bird is fast. So is Captain Neilson."

The captain laughed. "Don't I know it!"

"Are you both Amazons?" I asked.

"Not me, baby cakes," Captain Neilson said as she piloted the helicopter toward our destination.

"Captain Neilson is the best pilot in the world," the blonde Amazon said. "We hire her special." She stuck out her hand. "I'm Phoebe."

I shook, my eyes going to the golden crystal around her throat. I swallowed hard, reminded of everything at stake. I couldn't fail at this, for so many reasons.

"What do you know about the Garden of Hesperides?" Maximus asked.

"Well, don't eat the oranges, for one," Phoebe said. "You'll regret that for sure. And it's a big place, hard to find your way around." She spent a little while describing the terrain, and I did my best to visualize it.

"Nearly there!" Captain Neilson said. "Get your harnesses on!"

"Harnesses?" I frowned.

"We can't land." Phoebe tossed me a harness, and I snagged it out of the air. "So we'll lower you down into the garden."

I grinned, liking the sound of that. *Definitely* James Bond. I glanced at Maximus, expecting him to look even greener. Instead, he looked more relaxed.

"You don't mind?" I asked.

"As long as I'm not in this tin can, I'm delighted."

"So, dangling from the tin can as it hovers a hundred feet over the ground is better?"

"Much." He smiled and strapped the harness around his waist and legs. "I can tolerate that, but it's just unnatural to fly."

"You can take the boy out of Ancient Rome, but you can't take Ancient Rome out of the boy," I said.

"Rome?" Phoebe said. "You're Roman?"

"Hell no," Maximus said. "Despite my name, I'm sure as hell not Roman. Germanic, first century AD."

"Fucking Romans. Copycats, the lot of them," Phoebe said.

I grinned, laughing. Ancient grudges died hard, and Romans were notorious for copying the Greeks.

"We're here!" Captain Neilson stopped the helicopter so it hovered in midair.

I moved toward the door, which Phoebe pushed open. She grabbed the line attached to my harness and fed it into some kind of mechanical device that I assumed would help lower me to the ground. She pushed the button so the machine started to whir, and I leaned out over the edge, getting ready to drop.

She met my eyes right as I lowered myself out. "Oh, and beware of Ladon."

I was already descending on the line when she said the name. I looked up at her. "What's Ladon?"

"A dragon," she shouted down after me.

My stomach dropped. "What? A dragon!"

She just grinned. "Good luck!"

I was too far down to ask any more questions. The wind whipped at my hair as the line lowered me to the forest below. If it was a garden, it was a big one. A wild one. No rose bushes and benches for quiet reading in here.

I glanced up to see Maximus following, a relaxed grin on his face. Weirdo. My stomach was doing the jitterbug.

Branches scraped at me as I descended through the trees. When my feet hit the ground below, I yanked off the harness and gave it a tug. It ascended back through the trees.

Maximus landed next to me and made quick work of removing his harness. He gave it a tug so Phoebe got the cue, and it rose up through the trees. A moment later, the sound of the helicopter drifted away.

I turned in a circle, inspecting the forest around us. "It's an orchard."

Thousands of oranges hung from the trees, their scent intoxicating. I itched to reach out and pick one. Scowling, I shoved my hand into my pocket. Not only were Phoebe's warnings echoing in my ears, but I could just *feel* that it would be a bad idea to eat these oranges. Eating the food of the gods was always risky, particularly when it hung from a tree.

"Any idea which way to go?" Maximus asked.

"Not a clue." I looked around, but saw no animals or people. "Let's see if we can find a clue or a person. Something."

Together, we moved quietly through the forest. I kept my senses on high alert, ready for anything to dart out. In the distance, the sound of water roared.

"A river," I said. "Maybe a waterfall."

"Loud enough to be a waterfall."

Ahead of us, a massive pile of black dirt glittered in the sunlight. Were there diamonds in it? My heart picked up speed. I'd never been one for the glitter really, but a massive pile of diamonds would pique anyone's interest.

I picked up my pace toward the dirt, my gaze running over it with interest. Only once it began to move did I realize that it was not, in fact, a pile of dirt studded with diamonds.

Nope. It was alive.

My stomach lurched, and I stumbled backward, right into Maximus.

Before we could get out of the way, the pile of dirt swung its head toward us, flaming red eyes pinning me in their sights.

Holy fates, the dragon.

The beast was huge, with glittering black scales and enormous wings folded along its back like it'd been catnapping in the orange grove. Its neck was long and graceful, its head angular and narrow. Black spikes extended off the back of it, each threaded through with red fire. They tapered off near the wings, which flared upward.

"Ladon," I whispered, awed.

The beast reared its head back as if to strike, mouth opening to reveal onyx fangs and a brilliant red tongue.

Would it barbecue me first?

The dragon's nose twitched. The flames in its eyes banked, and it tilted its head, curious. Then it leaned forward and sniffed me, drawing in my scent.

Sister.

The words echoed in my mind. "Did you say that?"

Sister.

"Sort of, yes," I said. "I'm a DragonGod."

The beast nodded its head, as if understanding. Hell, who was I kidding? Of course it understood. It probably understood the secrets of the universe.

"We're looking for the daughters of Atlas. The Hesperides. Do you know where we might find them?"

The dragon shrugged an elegant shoulder, one wing lifting up in the process. *Can take you part way.*

"Oh, thank you!" I turned to Maximus, smiling.

He was looking between me and the dragon, a slight grin on his face.

The dragon raised its front leg, gesturing with its claws for me to raise my hand and present it, palm up. Somehow, it was easy to read his intentions, even though he didn't speak. I did as he asked, turning my right palm upward.

He reached out with his main claw and poked my index finger hard. Pain shot through me, but I didn't move my hand as bright blood beaded on the surface of my skin.

The dragon pierced one of his own fingers, which looked much more reptilian than human, and pressed his bloody appendage to mine. Though it was generally a bad idea to mix blood with another—I wasn't a moron—this was a *dragon*. And the air cracked with magic.

No way I was going to miss out on whatever this was.

As the dragon's blood flowed into me, something inside me seemed to settle down. To be at peace. It almost felt as if I weren't fighting what was inside me. Even the dark magic.

Whoa.

I sucked in a deep breath. This was awesome.

The dark magic was in there, but somehow, it wasn't quite as dark as it had been. Like it had absorbed some goodness from the dragon or something. It made it easier to accept that it was there, at least.

Embrace your magic.

Prometheus's words echoed through my mind, excavating themselves from beneath the drunken stupor that had hidden them away.

Was this what he had meant?

Though he'd also told me to beware the dragon. I remembered that now. Or had he really said beware? Or just keep an eye out?

Whatever it was, I was so damned glad I'd met Ladon. I grinned at him. "Thanks."

I wasn't quite sure what he'd done—not exactly. But I knew it had helped me. I'd never felt so at peace. Like it really was easier to embrace what was inside me.

The dragon lowered himself toward the forest floor, holding out one of his front legs to form a step.

"Thanks." I turned to Maximus. "We need to climb on. He's giving us a ride part way."

"You can speak dragon?"

"I can speak Ladon, at least." I grinned and climbed onto the dragon. If I'd thought climbing into a helicopter on top of a roof was cool, that was nothing compared to this.

Ladon's scales were smooth and warm, and I found a seat in between his wings. Maximus sat behind me, and I turned to smile back at him. Joy filled me like a hot air balloon, threatening to carry me away.

Ladon crouched low, then leapt into the air, his wings carrying us high over the trees. I laughed, unable to keep it inside, as the wind tore at my hair and we swept over the Garden of the Hesperides.

There was literally nothing in the whole wide world quite like riding a dragon.

Ladon carried us high over the ground, gliding past rivers and meadows and lakes. The Garden of the Hesperides was massive—a world unto itself, hidden away from humans, where a dragon could live and fly free.

Elation surged through me as he soared, and I tried to imprint every second of it on my brain. When he slowed and descended toward a river, I was so happy from the ride that it was impossible to be disappointed that it was over.

He landed lightly on the ground, and I climbed off, letting Maximus go first so I could have one more second on the dragon. I'd have lived here, if he'd let me.

Once I was on the ground, I walked around to the front of Ladon. "Thank you."

He inclined his head, then reached for his shoulder and pulled off a scale. The shiny black thing was about the size of my palm, shot through with red. He handed it to me. *Follow the river to the Hesperides.*

I took it and nodded, unsure of what it was for but not about to turn down a gift from a dragon. "Thank you again."

Go with fire. And embrace your gifts. Even the frightening ones. Especially those.

I nodded, determined to do as he said. To lose my fear and become the badass I had to be.

Ladon crouched low once again and leapt into the sky, his wings carrying him away so fast that I barely had a chance to say goodbye to his retreating form.

I turned to Maximus. "Whoa. That was just whoa."

He nodded. "It's the only word for it, really. Did he tell us where to go next?"

"We have to follow the river." I looked down at the dragon scale in my hand, which had begun to burn. Soon, it was so hot that it singed my fingers.

I dropped it, unable to hold it any longer, and gaped as magic sparked around it, causing the scale to duplicate. Over and over, until it formed a small boat that glittered black and diamond like the dragon, with hints of red shot through.

"Holy fates." I gaped at the boat, which had to be ten feet long and contained two benches upon which to sit. There were no oars, but the current in the river was so strong that it might not be a problem.

"A dragon scale boat." Maximus shook his head. "Amazing. When Virtus, the god of battle, gave me my magic, I thought I'd seen it all. I was wrong."

"I don't think we've seen half of it." Tentatively, I leaned down and laid my hand on the boat. It was cool to the touch. I looked up at Maximus. "Ready to do this?"

He nodded. Together, we shoved the boat toward the river. Once it floated, we climbed inside and pushed away from shore. Immediately, the boat navigated its way to the middle of the water, no oars needed.

"Amen for dragon boats." I relaxed, enjoying the journey down the river.

Trees rushed by on either side, enormous old oaks and aspens and laurels. All kinds, really, and I couldn't help but think of the myths where nymphs and other beautiful women ran away from men, and their only escape was to be turned into trees. What a crap deal for them.

I scowled, suddenly reminded of the danger of this place.

Up ahead, the river seemed to disappear into nowhere. The trees, too.

I squinted. "What's that?"

Maximus cocked his head, clearly listening. "Do you hear that? The roar of water?"

I did, finally. And *holy fates.* Understanding hit me. I turned to Maximus, knowing my eyes were as wide as saucers. "A waterfall. We're headed straight toward a waterfall."

His face paled as his eyes stayed riveted to the river in front of us. "It's too late."

I turned back. He was right. We were already there, as if the boat had sped up, anxious to plunge us toward our deaths.

The bow of the boat tipped over the edge of the waterfall, and I looked down, hundreds of feet toward the pool below.

Holy fates, we were dead.

CHAPTER EIGHT

As the boat plummeted toward the pool below, the scream died in my throat, killed by the wind and sheer terror. Water rushed around us as we fell, the waterfall roaring. I clung to the boat, unable to look back at Maximus to see if he was still there.

Why had Ladon sent us this way?

There was no time to contemplate as we fell. Seconds passed, the longest of my life as my stomach leapt into my throat and my skin iced with fear.

Embrace your power.

Hell yeah, I had to embrace it. *Right now.*

I had power over water, thanks to Poseidon, and if I was ever going to use it, now was the time.

I reached deep inside me for the water magic, finding it easily now that Ladon had given me a drop of his blood. It surged within me, feeling cold and wet against my insides, and I forced the magic outward, commanding the river below to rise up.

It happened quickly, more quickly than it ever had before, and the waterfall rose, forming a gradual slope. My muscles ached and my breaths heaved. Manipulating the magic was a physical task as well as a mental one, and damn, was I feeling it.

The boat rose up with the water, surging along amongst the waves that rushed us gradually downward.

"You've got it!" Maximus shouted. "Keep going!"

His voice was a balm on my soul. I couldn't see him, but hearing him... He was alive. Still here, thank fates, not fallen to his death on the rocks below.

The horrible thought almost made me lose control of the water, distracting me from the magic. The wave beneath us wobbled, and we were still at least a hundred feet from the real river below.

I shook away the awful visions and focused on my magic, controlling the water and keeping us alive. Gradually, we glided lower, following the slope of the waterfall down toward the main river. When the hull of our boat touched the natural water, I sagged, grateful. A massive splash sounded from behind us as the rest of the water fell, sending up a wave that pushed us forward.

"Crap!" I clung to the seat as the boat rocked along with the waves. Finally, we drifted to a calmer pace. I sagged, looking at Maximus. "You okay?"

"Fine. Well done, there."

"Thanks." I trembled from adrenaline, and I felt like a limp noodle.

We floated down a wide, deep river that flowed more slowly than the one above. On either side, the bank was flat and peaceful, covered with long grass that waved in the wind. The watery sun was filtered through clouds, and the light breeze that blew my hair back from my face smelled of a spring meadow.

If we hadn't just plunged to our almost-deaths, I'd have called it a lovely afternoon.

"Any idea when we should stop the boat?" Maximus asked.

"Nope. Ladon didn't say." I squinted ahead at a spot where the water rippled slightly. "You see that?"

"The water is moving. There's something in it."

My muscles tightened.

Oh, crap.

No way it was friendly. Not with our luck.

Whatever it was moved quickly toward us, pushing up the water in front of it. The mound of water grew and grew, until a massive head burst forth.

Green scales, a huge mouth filled with fangs, and bulbous eyes.

My heart slammed against my rib cage.

"A sea monster," Maximus said.

Cetus.

The word echoed in my head. "It's the Cetus. A Greek sea monster."

And it was *massive.*

The thing was so big that it would swallow our boat whole. The mouth was at least ten feet across. Panic iced my veins as it neared, pushing through the water like a bulldozer.

It was only thirty feet off now. The inside of its mouth gleamed red and black, and I could just imagine us heading straight down its gullet.

My heart thundered as I looked to the shore. It was about fifteen feet away. Too far to jump. Too far to swim.

Behind me, Maximus stood.

He was strong as hell, so he could probably crush the life out of the beast if he could get a good enough grip. But what if the monster took him deep below the river? In the time it took to crush the life from him, Maximus could be lost under the water.

Seconds raced by as the monster neared. It reeked of fish and dead bodies, and its milky white eyes never left us.

I needed to shock the hell out of this thing.

My magic was the only way.

It was still fifteen feet off.

I rose to my feet, calling upon the magic within me. "I've got this."

"No, let me," Maximus said.

I ignored him, and since I was in the front of the boat already, I had the advantage.

Lightning crackled through my veins as I gathered up the magic of Zeus. I'd love to throw a lightning bolt like Bree, but my specialty seemed to be of the human bomb variety. I felt like I was filled with a thousand volts of electricity, and I was ready to light up that fish.

I climbed onto the bow, my eyes on the Cetus, which was almost to us. I embraced Zeus's magic, which sparked within me, lightning coursing through my muscles.

The plan was insane, but we were still only about fifteen feet from shore. So it could work.

Please work.

Right in front of our boat, the monster reared up, its mouth open wide and ready to strike. I leapt as high as I could. Shock flashed in its white eyes as I jumped toward the beast.

Ha! I bet prey never jump right at it.

I grabbed onto the monster's lower lip. The beast shrieked as I touched it, my lightning coursing through its body. I tightened my hands, determined not to let go. The monster thrashed in the water, its head still raised high as it lit up like the Fourth of July. Pain tore through my muscles, too, and it took everything I had to cling to the Cetus.

Fates, I hated this power.

Beneath me, the water surged and roiled. I couldn't see Maximus, but prayed he was still in the boat. I didn't want to fall into the water and electrocute him. He was impervious to most injury, but still...

Still hanging from the monster's lip, I began to swing left and right, trying to force my body weight toward the shore. The creature, vibrating from my electricity, swayed with me, then finally collapsed with its head on the shore.

I let go immediately, rolling aside and panting. The magic faded, taking the pain with it. My muscles melted as I lay in the grass next to the stinking Cetus. It wasn't dead, but stunned. No way I wanted to be lying there when it woke.

Aching, I dragged myself upright, searching the river for the boat.

Shock lanced me as I spotted the bottom half of the Cetus. It was a huge snake-like beast that was far bigger than I'd even realized. The bottom half of its tail stretched all the way across the river, bobbing on the surface and blocking the boat from traveling downstream. Hundreds of spikes ran down its back, each one black and glinting in the light. River water built up against the creature's body, and the empty boat was pressed against it.

Maximus had jumped onto the Cetus's long body and was running toward me and the shore. He moved so fast I didn't have a chance to ask what he was doing.

Next to me, the Cetus blinked its milky eyes. It opened and closed its mouth once, then twice. Then faster and faster, like it was trying to eat the air. Giant nostrils quivered as it caught my scent, and it wriggled to try to get to me.

I lunged backward, stumbling against a lump of dirt and going to my butt. Panicked, I scrambled upright and ran from the monster. It wasn't as fast on land, but it moved toward me unerringly, its mouth constantly opening and closing, as if it were determined to get a bite of me.

It was an eating machine with breath like dead bodies.

I could light it up with electricity again, but I really didn't want to. My muscles still ached like hell.

When Maximus reached the shore, he leapt onto the grass and grabbed one of the long spikes that stuck up off of the Cetus's back. Then he pulled, his muscles straining and veins popping.

The creature was so huge that it had to weigh two thousand pounds, but he yanked it across the grass, dragging it away from me and out of the water entirely.

Water that had built up behind the monster's body poured forward, rushing down the river.

Maximus had dragged the creature entirely out of the river, but it was still moving. The head was still chomping, and it was pretty damn spry for having just been electrocuted. It could probably wriggle back into the river if it really tried.

Maximus let go of the monster's back spike and sprinted to the tail. He grabbed it and dragged it to the monster's head. Quickly, he shoved the tail into the mouth. Fangs chomped down on the tail, and the monster didn't even flinch. Then it chomped some more.

"Moron." I sprinted toward Maximus.

"Hurry! The boat is fast."

He was right. It drifted away from us on the current about twenty yards ahead. I joined him, and we raced for it. My muscles ached and my legs wobbled, but I pushed hard, desperate to reach the boat that the dragon had given us.

We sprinted through the waving grass, gaining on the boat. It was about twenty feet from shore, so way too far to jump.

Damn it, we needed it closer.

As if the boat had heard me, it veered toward shore.

"Are you doing that?" Maximus asked.

"I think so." I panted, running toward the water as the boat pulled up alongside us.

When it was only a couple feet away, I jumped and landed in a pile in the bottom of the boat. As quickly as I could, I scooted out of the way so Maximus could join me. He jumped in far more gracefully and landed in an elegant crouch.

Gasping, I scrambled onto a bench as the boat rocked. It veered back toward the middle of the river. My muscles trembled.

"Nice work with the human lightning bolt," Maximus said.

"Thanks." I grinned. "I like how you turned him into an Ouroboros."

"He just wouldn't stop biting."

"Miserable beast." I peered back toward the monster, which was currently still eating its own tail. "I guess he doesn't care what he eats."

Maximus grinned and pulled me to him, pressing a kiss to my forehead. I leaned into him, absorbing his warmth and strength.

But just for a moment.

This place was far too dangerous for any distractions.

I pulled back and turned to face the water.

"How did Zeus's magic feel?" Maximus asked. "Are you getting it under control?"

"I think." I nodded. "It felt better this time than last time. Easier to call to the surface. And it hurt, but not as badly. And at least it didn't explode out of me." Like it had in class.

I didn't mention that bit, though.

Ahead, the water rippled again. I pointed toward it, exhaustion snaking through my bones. Whatever was coming, I didn't want to fight it.

"The ripples are smaller, at least." I squinted, trying to see what was beneath the river.

As it neared, a head broke through the surface of the water. A beautiful woman, with a crown of red coral sitting on her gleaming blonde hair. White silk waved around her in the river, and she turned to us and smiled. She was still about twenty yards away, but I could sense no threat from her. No dark magic.

"Hello!" I called.

She smiled wider and swam closer. "You defeated the Cetus."

"Miserable jerk," I said.

"He was such a menace." She kept pace with our boat easily, though I could see no legs or fins beneath the water. "What are you doing here in the Garden of Hesperides?"

"Looking for the Hesperides, actually." I grinned. "I'm Rowan. And this is Maximus."

"I am Actaia, a Nereid."

I frowned, searching my memory for the term. "A sea nymph?"

It seemed as good a guess as any.

Her smile lit up her whole face, and she really was pretty. "Precisely. We are part of Poseidon's entourage. We symbolize everything that is beautiful and kind about the sea." She laughed and spun in the water, a vision of pure joy. Sure, she was a bit nuts, but she seemed nice and that was all that mattered.

"Why are you in a river if you symbolize the sea?" Maximus asked.

She scowled a bit. "It was getting crowded in the Aegean. There are a lot of us, you know."

"So you struck out on your own," Maximus said.

She beamed. "Yes, exactly. I wanted adventure."

I hiked a thumb back toward the Cetus. "Well, you'll get it here."

She scowled in the direction of the monster. "He was the bane of my existence. Always swimming around, looking for something to eat. Preferably me."

"Now he's out of your hair." I glanced back at the Cetus, who had almost disappeared from view. He was still eating his tail. "Looks like he'll be busy for a while."

She smiled again—she was literally the smiliest girl I'd ever met—but this grin was tinged with evil glee. "Yes, that was clever."

"Is there any chance you could help us find the Hesperides?" I asked.

She turned to me, her blue eyes glinting. "I'd be delighted. I've taken it upon myself to perform a Nereid's duties upon this river."

"Thank you." I smiled. "It would be very kind of you to show us the way."

"Indeed." She inclined her head, then grabbed onto the bow of the boat. "Come, I will show you the way."

She pulled us along, surprisingly strong for such a normal-sized woman. Fish. Woman-fish. Whatever.

I glanced at Maximus and shrugged, smiling.

The boat moved more quickly with her help. As she swam, she began to sing. At one point, she looked over her shoulder. "Our voices are very melodious, aren't they?"

"Very." Yep, she was a bit odd, but I liked odd.

"The dragon Ladon must have favored you if he gave you this boat," she said.

"What does he do here?" I asked.

"He guards the grove. Be sure to take the boat with you when you go. This is a wondrous gift."

Take it with me?

She veered toward shore.

"We're here!" She shoved the boat onto the shore, then smiled. "Head away from the river directly. I must be off, now. Safe travels."

With that, she plunged into the river, gone as quickly as

she'd come. I didn't even have a chance to ask about taking the boat with me.

I turned to Maximus. "Well, that was a lucky break."

"That's the truth." He jumped out of the boat and pulled it onto the shore with ease.

I climbed out, grateful to be on solid ground. As soon as my second foot left the boat, it began to collapse. The scales folded in on themselves until the boat had returned to its original size of just one scale. It sat in the grass, glinting black and diamond.

"Whoa." I bent to pick it up, inspecting it. "Freaking amazing."

"The dragon chose you," Maximus said. "It believed in you."

I met his gaze. "I don't know if that should make me feel so good, but damned if it isn't awesome."

He grinned.

I tucked the scale into my pocket and turned to survey the land around us. The field gave way to forest in the distance, and I pointed to it. "Since Actaia said to head directly away from the river, I bet she meant to go toward that forest."

"Let's go quickly, then. The sun is getting low."

I glanced toward it. We only had a couple of hours of daylight left. Three, at most. "Yeah, I want to be out of here by nightfall."

As soon as I stepped away from the river, the comms charm at my neck vibrated with magic.

"Rowan? You there?" Bree's voice whispered out.

"I am. Safe to talk."

"Good." Her voice came through louder this time. "We've got an update. Hedy found a spell that allowed us to see through the barrier."

"But not break through?" I cut in.

"Unfortunately, no. But we saw the Stryx. They're both in there, along with an army of almost a hundred."

"A hundred?" *Shit.*

"Mostly demons. They're helping them dig into the earth, like we thought. Explosives mostly, and some magic."

"Damn."

"With that many workers, they'll move fast," Maximus said. "Did you get any clue as to what they're after?"

"No," Bree said. "Can't see that far. And since we haven't found a way to break through the barrier, we're counting on you, Rowan."

I swallowed hard, the pressure settling on my shoulders like a heavy cape. "I'm on it. I think we're getting close."

"Good luck, then. And be safe. We'll keep you updated."

"Likewise. Love you."

"Love you." She cut the connection, and the magic in my comms charm fell dormant.

I looked at Maximus. "Let's hurry."

We strode across the field, grass waving against our legs as birds chirped from the sky above. It was all so lovely. I didn't trust it.

The forest itself was creepier, the trees casting a dark shadow within. A layer of dead leaves crunched underfoot as we stepped inside. The air changed, growing cooler without the light of the sun. A protection charm prickled against my skin, and I'd bet big bucks it meant we couldn't transport in or out of this place.

I veered closer to Maximus, who reached for my hand.

"The Romans believed the forest was dark and full of terrors," Maximus said.

"They might have been right." I shivered as a tree branch scraped across my arm.

"I'm not sure they were. Their cities were bad enough."

"Good point."

"To them, the forest represented the unknown. But to me, it

was escape. When I was in the Colosseum, I dreamed of the forests of my home."

My heart ached for him. "Did you ever see them again?"

He shook his head. "They were gone by the time I escaped and was sent forward in time. Which is fine. It wasn't the forest so much as the freedom that I wanted."

"So you're not scared here?"

He looked at me, his gaze calm. "I'm not scared much of anywhere. Nothing compares to the Colosseum."

"Except helicopters."

A smile broke out across his face. "Exactly. Helicopters are the devil himself."

I laughed.

What's so funny?

Romeo's voice sounded from my feet, and I looked down. He trotted alongside us, with Eloise and Poppy next to him.

I smiled. "When did you get here?"

Just now. Danger coming.

"Danger?"

"What danger?" Maximus asked.

"Romeo says danger is coming." I looked down at the raccoon. "What kind?"

Don't know. Just felt it.

Well, shit. That wasn't good. I stayed alert, inspecting the forest as we walked. We were still headed away from the river as Actaia had suggested, but I had no idea if we were getting close. The forest all looked the same.

It was silent except for our footsteps. Maybe too silent.

The hair on my arms stood on end as we walked. I couldn't hear the threat, but I could feel it.

"Do you feel that?" I whispered.

"The forest doesn't like us," Maximus murmured.

"Or something in the forest." I peered through the trees, trying to spot anything that was a threat.

The Menacing Menagerie skulked along, their fur raised on their backs as they warily eyed the forest.

A sense of deep unease washed over me, along with the feeling of being watched. My skin prickled under the weight of dozens of eyes. I *knew* there were dozens. They lurked in the forest.

We neared a clearing where the trees were particularly fat and gnarled. They looked like sentries guarding a place I never wanted to enter.

"Let's go around this part," I said.

"I like that plan."

We moved left, but a low growl sounded.

I stopped in my tracks, my muscles tense.

"Who's there?" Maximus demanded.

The growl came again, followed by another. And another. Soon, there were dozens, the sounds coming from all around. But I couldn't see them.

Animals. Not monsters. Romeo arched his back, his gray hair standing upright. Eloise hissed, puffing up her fur. Poppy pulled back her lips, revealing little fangs.

From behind the trees, animals crept out.

Wolves and stags, bears and large forest cats. Dozens of them. They surrounded us in a circle, all growling. All with their eyes on us.

All looking a hell of a lot like they wanted to eat us.

I swallowed hard.

Shit, we were screwed.

CHAPTER NINE

There were so damned many.

How were we supposed to fight them all?

We couldn't. If they charged, we couldn't take them all on. Not to mention, I wasn't keen on killing a bunch of forest creatures, even if they were in a bad mood and wanted to kill me back.

Maximus and I stood shoulder to shoulder, each vibrating with tension. My fingertips itched to draw a blade, but I didn't want to show any signs of aggression.

I've got this.

I looked down at Romeo, who had flattened his fur in an attempt to not look scared. "What do you mean?"

Just watch. He walked toward the animals, then sat on his butt, holding up his front paws. *We come in peace.*

Two wolves in front of him lunged, teeth bared and growls low.

Whoa! Romeo darted back toward my legs.

The wolves stopped, their lips still up and their rumbles of aggression rolling through the forest. The fur at their backs stood straight up. Around them, the rest of the animals were poised to attack.

I don't think I've got this.

"It's okay, Romeo." I looked from him to the animals, suddenly very annoyed. "What the hell is your problem? We're just walking through."

They growled louder, and it just pissed me off even more. "Are you guarding something?"

More growls. I had no idea if they understood me, but I could feel their angst. They were pissed I was here. It was obvious, not just from the sounds they made, but from how they *felt.*

Hang on.

How they felt?

Was I feeling what they were feeling?

Magic prickled through me, filling me up with a sparkling sensation of *knowing.* Like I was connected to the animals.

You are.

I blinked.

The voice sounded in my head again. *Command them.*

Holy fates, I was getting another DragonGod power. From a goddess this time, if the tone of the voice was any indication. Artemis, I had to assume. She was goddess of the hunt. She held dominion over the animals of the forest.

The animals prowled closer, fangs and claws glinting. They did protect something in this forest, though I had no idea what. The Hesperides?

"Stop it." I imbued my voice with command.

They just growled louder.

Embrace your magic.

I called upon the new magic that bubbled within me. It was a less aggressive power, more elusive. It floated through my being like smoke, hard to grab ahold of. So I didn't fight it.

Instead, I let it fill me, relaxing my whole body and embracing the idea that I could share a connection with the animals.

I already felt their annoyance with me. I wanted to feel more. Their hopes and desires and fears. I wanted them to feel connected to me as well, so they'd listen to me.

Slowly, Artemis's magic filled me. As it did, my hearing improved. Suddenly, I could hear heartbeats beneath the growls. I could smell warm fur and musk over the aroma of fallen leaves.

Was I getting the powerful senses of some of these animals? Jackpot.

There were at least thirty of them here. I didn't need to count —I could feel their life forces, connected to mine.

"Stop growling," I said. "We're not here to hurt anyone."

The growls slowed, but didn't cease. I reached for the magic that had filled me and pushed some of it out toward them. Instead of moving powerfully, like most of my magic did, it drifted calmly on the air. There was a faint sparkle to it, and it rolled over the animals. As it passed them, they relaxed, their fur flattening out and their growls ceasing.

They still looked at me with wary eyes, but they seemed to get my point. We really weren't here to mess with anyone. None of them stepped forward, wanting to be friendly and let me act out my fantasies of being Snow White with a bunch of forest friends, but at least they weren't attacking.

Now what?

I looked down at Romeo. "No idea. I don't think they'll attack."

"They won't, as long as you keep control of them." The feminine voice came with a good dose of godly power. It rolled over me, making my insides shake.

I turned, catching sight of a tall woman wearing a knee-

103

length white dress. It flowed easily around her, made of minimal fabric and with no frills that would get in the way. A golden bow was strapped across her back, along with a quiver of arrows. Her dark hair was tied back from her face.

"Artemis?" I stepped forward.

She nodded. "Indeed. And you must be Rowan, the DragonGod."

"I am. Thank you for giving me your power."

"You fight for a worthy cause." Her assessing gaze traveled to Maximus. "And you travel with a worthy companion."

"I couldn't do it without him."

"Perhaps you could, but not as quickly and not as easily. You make a good team." Her gaze moved back to me. "But you haven't fully embraced your magic, yet."

"I used my lightning. And my water gift. And the one from you."

"But not the gift of Hades. The one that you fear."

My cheeks burned. "No."

"The magic of the gods can sense your fear. You must overcome it if you wish to succeed. Prove yourself, here in this forest, or you will never achieve your goals."

"I have to succeed. The Amazons need me. The world needs me."

"Then prove you aren't afraid."

"How?"

"Use the magic. Use it with confidence and make it yours. No more cringing back." She smiled. "Now be careful in the forest. It is a dangerous place, even for a DragonGod."

With that, she disappeared.

I turned to Maximus. "I think she showed up just to give me a lecture."

His lips quirked up at the corners. "It seems so. But she has a point. You're the bravest person I've ever met, Rowan. You don't need to be afraid of your magic. You can control it. You've done it before."

I swallowed and nodded, knowing he was right. It wasn't regular, healthy fear that I was feeling. It was a holdover from my time with the Rebel Gods.

"When I was a captive of the Rebel Gods, I was swallowed by their dark magic. I don't want that to happen again. Not with the dark magic that is inside me. I can't go back to that."

"You won't have to. You can control it."

I *had* to. I needed this magic to save the Amazons and to save that village from the Stryx.

Wimping out wasn't really an option.

"Okay. I've got my act together." I looked at the animals who still surrounded us, their gazes calm and waiting. "Lead us to the Hesperides, please."

I made my voice firm, but polite. The animals would know every inch of their forest, so I might as well use their expertise.

As a group, they bowed their heads, then turned and began to walk slowly through the trees.

Nice trick. Romeo gave me a thumbs-up. *I'd like to be boss like that.*

I chuckled and followed the animals, Maximus at my side. As we walked, my newly improved animal hearing picked up on the dozens of heartbeats all around. I heard the slight whistle of the wind through the trees and the crunch of leaves beneath a wolf's paw.

This was badass.

Slowly, I drew in air through my nose, focusing on the different scents. Dirt, leaves, grass, fur, water. I could pick out each, and it was incredible. Of all the new powers I'd been given, I might like this one the best.

The animals led us through the trees for a while. With every mile we walked, the sky seemed to grow a little darker. It wasn't night yet, but it was close.

When we entered a clearing, I stopped abruptly, gasping at the sight within.

A castle made of thorns occupied the space, the dying yellow sunlight making it gleam like a deadly trap. It was about a quarter of the size of the Protectorate castle, which made it still pretty big.

"What is this place?"

"It looks like it's been here a long time," Maximus answered.

Slowly, I approached it. The thorns were pale and sharp, all of them protruding off of thick vines that looked almost dead.

I turned to a wolf who had stopped next to me. "Are you sure this is it?"

He stared intently at the structure, standing stock still.

He seems sure. Romeo touched it, then shivered and withdrew his hand. Eloise and Poppy were too smart to even bother.

"The Hesperides must be inside." My gaze traveled over the entire thing, and I frowned. "Did it grow up around them?"

The animals gave me no clue.

"What if the vines have grown through the doors and windows? If we try to break our way in, we could pull the wrong vine and hurt the Hesperides," Maximus said. "Move one vine the wrong way, and the thorns could stab them."

He was right. This was a delicate operation.

I reached out and gripped the vine with my hand. They looked dead, but life flowed through them.

We needed the vines to remove themselves, withering away harmlessly.

There was one way to do that.

I swallowed hard, dread uncoiling within me.

Carefully, I drew in a steady breath, forcing the dread away. I still felt it, but I could pretend I didn't. Mostly.

"I think I can do it," I said.

Maximus squeezed my arm, understanding. "You're strong, Rowan. You'll be fine."

I nodded, my gaze glued to the vines. I'd done this before, when my life was at stake. I'd been fine. I could do it again. Especially when *other* people's lives were at stake.

I trembled, tightening my grip on the vine. I just had to access the death magic. That was all. Not the darkness from the Rebel Gods or any old nightmares. Just Hades's death magic.

It was natural. Right?

Take their power. Use it. Send them to the underworld. The words that Hades had once whispered in my head echoed through me.

When I'd practiced the magic before—the one time, on the plant in Maximus's house—I'd imagined my death magic as residing in a bottle with a stopper. I did the same this time, carefully uncorking the bottle in my mind. The magic hesitated at first, as if it knew I didn't want it.

I didn't.

But I needed it. And life wasn't always about getting what you wanted.

Come on.

I reached for the magic, envisioning sucking the life from this plant so it would wither away. The magic rose up within me, dark and bright, like it had been before. It seemed like an impossible concept, but it wasn't.

This wasn't necessarily an evil power, but it sucked.

I drew in a shuddery breath and directed the magic toward the plant. Sweat dripped down my temples, and my muscles shook as I carefully fueled the death magic into the plant. I didn't want it exploding out of me like the lightning had, killing anyone it touched.

Before my eyes, the vine began to wither. It shrunk in on itself, flowing out of the plant and into me. I grew stronger as it happened, feeling like a parasite. A *strong* parasite.

Damn, I could probably lift a car right now. Though I hated stealing the energy, there was one positive aspect. It made it easier to control my magic. I funneled more and more of the death magic into the vine, taking its life in return. The idea made me slightly queasy, but my muscles felt great. I was no longer trembling or sweating.

Fates, if I didn't have a conscience, this could become addictive.

The vines withered faster and faster, shrinking on themselves until they began to crumble away. The structure beneath was made of marble. Beautiful columns surrounded a temple, deep in the forest. They were dull with age and lack of care, but the building itself was sound.

"You've almost got it," Maximus said.

I fed a bit more magic into the last of the vines, forcing them to wither and draw back. Finally, the last of them faded away. I removed my hand with a gasp. Energy flowed through me, strength and power. I felt like I'd had a twelve-hour nap and a good breakfast.

I turned to Maximus. "I don't like that power."

"It's not evil."

"But it's not fair. I shouldn't take the life from other things." I looked at the remains of the withered vines. "It had to be done here. Those vines were trapping the Hesperides. But I don't like being the one to make the call. Even if they are just plants." *Because what if they aren't just plants?*

Maximus squeezed my arm gently, and he didn't need to speak to convey his thoughts.

Someone always had to make the hard call. And sometimes, that someone would be me.

Well, I'd done it. And I was going to forget it.

I turned to the animals. "Thank you for your help."

The crowd of predators stared at me, some inclining their heads.

"You may go."

They turned and disappeared into the forest. Okay, so I wasn't Snow White. They weren't volunteering to do my chores or sing a duet with me. At best, I had their begrudging allegiance. Since the alternative was them trying to eat me, I'd take it.

"Let's get inside before it's dark," Maximus said. "I don't think we'll like this forest in the dark."

I shivered. He had a point. The animals might not attack us, but there was plenty of dangerous magic here.

I looked down at Romeo, Poppy, and Eloise. "Thanks for coming, guys. Don't feel like you have to stick around."

We'll see what kind of trash they've got, then we'll bail.

I grinned. "Fair enough."

I turned and followed Maximus up the steps that led to the temple. There were only three, but they were wide and grand. Eight marble columns bordered the front of the building, and the massive door that led to the inside was an intricately carved wood. Three maidens danced upon it, surrounded by the light of the setting sun.

The door creaked as Maximus pulled it open, and I'd bet twenty bucks it weighed hundreds of pounds.

We stepped into a massive empty room. Another collection of thorns sat in the middle of the space. It was a pile about ten feet tall and eight feet wide, the vines twisted over each other in a horrible knot.

"Shit." The space was so quiet that my words echoed off the walls. "There's no one in here." I eyed the thorns with dread.

"They're in there," Maximus said, pointing to the thorny mass. "Why would it be there, otherwise?"

I shivered as I stopped in front of the thorns, feeling the dark magic that radiated from them. Someone had put a curse on the Hesperides, trapping them within this horrible little prison. I prayed I'd find them alive.

I didn't hesitate this time, though I still didn't like it. I pressed my fingertip to one of the thorns. It was easier to call upon the magic inside me, feeding death into the wicked plant.

The vines withered quickly, breaking away to reveal three frozen figures, trapped for ages in a state of shock. The Hesperides were beautiful, three women in bright white dresses trimmed in gold. Dead roses were twined in their hair, and their faces were frozen in an expression of shock and horror. One had brown hair, one blonde, and the last had hair of flames.

The dark magic that I'd felt earlier surrounded them, trapping them. As the last of the vines withered away to the ground, the magic snapped, blowing me backward on a rancid wind.

Coughing on the foul taste, I stumbled away, holding my hand up in front of my face. Maximus grabbed me and pulled me back farther.

When I lowered my arm, the vines and the magic were gone.

"You did it," Maximus murmured.

"What foul magic was that!?" shrieked the brunette. She dragged the dead roses out of her hair and spun in a circle, her gaze finally landing on us. She pointed. "You!"

"Yes?" I stepped forward, eyeing her warily. She was *pissed.*

Her two sisters shook themselves, tugging the dead roses out of their hair and glaring at me.

"You trapped us in there, you foul witch!" cried the irate woman.

"I didn't." I held up my hands. "I freed you."

She propped her hands on her hips. "You did not."

"Yeah, I did. If I'd trapped you in there, why would I have removed the thorns and stuck around?"

"Stuck around? What does this mean?" Her gaze traveled over my clothes. "And what are you *wearing*? That's *awful*."

I looked down at my jeans and boots. They were a bit battered, but my leather jacket was quite nice. And ages ago, I'd put on my Pink Power lipstick. It was probably mostly gone by now, but I wasn't looking that bad. "I kind of like it."

"It's...it's...the garb of a man!"

"Ahhhh. I get it." I shared a glance with Maximus, and he nodded, clearly on the same page. "How long have you been frozen for, do you think?"

"However long you put us in there for." The brunette stomped toward me, her brow scrunched over her pretty face. She was pissed and she wasn't about to hide it. Her two sisters followed her.

"It's the twenty-first century," I said. "And I'm wearing these clothes because that's what women wear now."

She stopped dead in her tracks, her jaw dropping. "The twenty-first?"

"Yes." I tugged out my cell phone and handed it to her. She took it and stared at it, confused. "That's a cell phone. If you're surprised by my jeans, then you'll definitely be surprised by that. It'll also convince you I'm right, I bet."

"What year do you remember last?" Maximus asked.

The shouty one was too busy staring at the phone, her brow scrunched.

"It is the year 1898, of course," said the blonde.

"It's definitely not." I frowned at her. "You've been trapped for over a hundred and twenty years."

"Ugh." Her blue eyes flashed with ire. "It had to be Demeter, that wicked hoyden. I knew she was angry with us."

The redhead turned irate eyes on her sisters. "I told you she was coming for vengeance. We never should have stolen her crop."

"At least she didn't kill you," I said.

The three of them scoffed at me.

"As if she'd *ever.*"

She'd trapped them for over a hundred years in thorny vines. The death thing didn't seem that out of the question to me, but I didn't argue. I needed them on my side.

I reached out and retrieved my phone from the brunette, who was still looking at it, dumbfounded.

She glanced up at me, her eyes clearing. "I don't know what is in that little box, but I do not like it."

"That's okay. Are you thirsty? Or hungry?" Maybe Maximus could conjure them something, because ignoring the fact that they'd been trapped for a hundred years without a snack seemed rude.

The Hesperides ignored me. "What do you want? Why did you free us?"

"I am Rowan. I'm a DragonGod and an Amazon. This is Maximus."

He inclined his head in greeting.

"What are those rats?" The brunette pointed to the corner, and I turned, spotting the Menacing Menagerie.

All three of them looked horrifically offended. Poppy's mouth was hanging open, which really wasn't a good look for a possum.

I turned back to the Hesperides. "Ah, they aren't rats. They are the Menacing Menagerie. Formerly the most famous all-animal circus troop in Europe, but now they are primarily interested in your rubbish."

Her brows rose. "Rubbish?"

"Yes, well, I suppose you don't have any, given the circumstances. They'll get over it." I stepped forward, trying to make my face look pleading. "I need your help, though. The world needs your help."

"The world?" The blonde seemed intrigued at that. So did her sisters.

"Yes." I explained about the Stryx and the Amazons and their father. How the satellites were so important to the human militaries, and if they failed, then war would inevitably break out. "And that's why we need to find Atlas."

The brunette leaned back and tapped her lip, then looked at her sisters. They didn't need to speak, but some kind of message passed between them, and they all agreed.

She turned back to me. "What will you give us?"

I stared at her, dumfounded. "What the heck? I just saved you from over one hundred years of captivity."

"Yes. That was then, this is now. And it seems you need something from us."

"The world needs something from *you*," Maximus said.

"But you're the ones asking, so we want something from *you*."

"Like what?" I asked.

She tapped her chin again. "Hmmm." Then she began to circle me, like I was prey.

I spun to follow her movements, not liking this one little bit.

"You've got quite a lot of power, DragonGod," she mused. "I think I'd like to see the moon."

"Um, okay?" I looked between her and her sisters, but they didn't clarify. And Maximus looked as confused as I was. The Menacing Menagerie couldn't provide any clarification since they'd bailed shortly after being called rats.

"Well, get to it." The brunette waved her hands in a *hurry up* gesture. The other two stared at me expectantly.

"You expect *me* to show you the moon? You're nuts."

"You have the power of Artemis, don't you? Well, get to it and show me the moon. The sun has just set, but the moon has not yet risen. Make it rise. Speed it up a bit."

Holy shit, she had to be kidding. There was no way I could move the moon. That was insane.

CHAPTER TEN

"You can't be serious." I stared at her, dumbfounded. "I can't possibly move the moon."

"You'd better."

I began to pace. WTF. This was nuts. Make the moon rise? "It'll be terrible for the tides. I can't just screw with the moon, assuming I even have the ability."

"Pshaw." She waved her hands, clearly not interested. "The moon is almost here. It won't be so bad, just give it a little nudge. We are the daughters of twilight, and it's been over a hundred years since we've seen the moon. I want to see the moon!" She sounded so irate that I expected her to stomp her foot.

I held up my hands. "Okay, okay. I'll try." This was insane, but so was she. And she clearly wasn't going to take no for an answer. "Let's go outside and get this show over with."

I really hoped the moon was close. I had no idea how to pull this off, but if I managed it, I really didn't want to screw with the tides too much.

We walked out onto the front steps of the temple. Dusk had fallen, turning the sky a moody gray. Night insects created a horrible orchestra that battered my newly sensitive ears.

"Prove yourself, DragonGod," said the blonde. "We're getting tired of waiting."

I turned to scowl at her. "Hold your horses. I'm getting there."

Jeez, this was bonkers.

I shook my head to try to ignore the infernal buzzing from the night insects and turned my gaze to the sky.

What the heck was I supposed to do? Shout at the moon? Yell at it that Artemis had given me her magic and that it needed to follow my orders?

Yeah, that wasn't going to work.

I pursed my lips.

I probably had to do this the way I did anything with magic. I sucked in a deep breath and reached inside of me, looking for the magic that Artemis had given me. It was probably my favorite gift, so it wasn't hard to find. It felt like a breath of fresh air and the warm fur of a friendly cat. It even glowed a bit, like the moon.

Just like with my water magic, I tried to feel the moon's presence. It took a while—and I could feel the unimpressed stares of the Hesperides the whole time—but finally, I thought I could sense it, right at the edge of the horizon.

It really *was* close.

Thank fates.

Using my magic, I called to the moon. It was almost impossible to understand how I was doing it, but I could *feel* it. Like it was part of me.

That didn't make it easy.

It felt like pushing the *Titanic* toward the iceberg. Sweat dripped down my temples as I worked, using my magic like a lasso to draw the moon up over the horizon. Strength and energy poured out of me, all of the life that I'd taken from the vines going into this job.

It didn't take long for my muscles to weaken and my posture to sag. But I could feel it working. Slowly, the moon rose over the horizon.

Tonight, it was huge and white, totally full.

From behind me, the Hesperides sighed, delight in the sound. They really did like the moon.

As soon as it was entirely over the horizon, I stopped, stumbling forward. Maximus caught me.

Panting, I looked up at him. "I really hope I didn't screw anything up."

He grinned. "You just moved it a little bit. And it was a worthy cause."

I turned to look at the Hesperides, who seemed happier than kids on Christmas morning. The moon glowed on their faces, and for a moment, I forgot what bitches they were.

I caught my breath and let them enjoy it for a minute. Weak, I leaned against Maximus, leeching off of him to keep myself standing.

Finally, the Hesperides turned to me.

The leader, who did most of the talking, gave me a begrudging smile. "That was pretty good, DragonGod. You might be worthy of your magic, after all."

"I sure hope I am." There was way too much riding on me for me to fail. "Can you tell us where Atlas is, now?"

"We can give you your first clue."

"Clue? That wasn't the bargain."

She shrugged. "Take it or leave it, because we *can't* tell you where he is. If he's sick like you say he is, then he's retreated to his fortress in Greece. It's the only place he feels safe."

"Then tell me where that is."

"We can't. Even we don't know. No one does, not unless they pass the test that proves they bear him no ill will."

Okay, I didn't like hearing that, but it made sense. "What is the test?"

"It's a bit of blood magic that sees into your truest intentions. We can tell you how to perform it. All you have to do is find a Blood Sorceress to help you conduct the spell. If you mean him no ill will, then his location will be revealed to you."

"I can work with that. What is the spell?"

"Wait here a moment, and we will fetch it."

The three of them disappeared back into the temple. My knees were so wobbly that they were about to give out, so I sank down onto the step. Maximus joined me, wrapping an arm around my shoulders.

"Well done, Rowan. I think you're doing the Greek gods proud."

"I hope so." Whatever reticence I'd had to use my magic was gone. They'd wanted me to embrace my magic, and I sure as heck had. I'd raised the moon, for fate's sake.

Exhausted, I leaned my head against Maximus's shoulder and gazed out at the forest. "I'm glad you're with me on this adventure."

He squeezed my shoulders. "Me too. We make a good team." He cleared his throat. "Honestly, this is the first time I've felt at home since I was taken from my farm when I was a kid."

"With me?"

"With you."

Wow, I—

The Hesperide's voice rang out from behind me. "Here it is!"

I turned to see her sweeping through the massive door with a small scroll in her hand, her sisters behind her. "We've written it all down for you. Just find someone to conduct the spell, and you'll have what you want—as long as your intentions are pure."

My muscles ached as I stood and took the scroll to inspect it. The list of ingredients and instructions looked legit, as far as I could tell. Since there was no way to test them here, I had to take their word for it.

"Thanks."

They didn't bother acknowledging my gratitude, just turned and retreated into the temple.

I grinned wearily and looked at Maximus. "Well, I guess that's that."

～

"They don't waste time, at least."

"Let's get out of here. Can we use a transport charm? I felt a protection charm at the entrance to the forest."

Maximus shook his head. "I felt it, too. I think we need to get out of the woods before we try. This place is sacred—to Artemis, I assume—and I don't think transporting is allowed."

"She'd want to know who comes and goes from her woods."

"Indeed, I do." The godly voice resonated with power, and I spun to find Artemis stepping out from between the trees.

"You did well here, DragonGod."

"Thank you."

"You must not pass through the forest at night. It is too dangerous."

"We need to stop the Stryx," I said.

"You cannot stop them if you are dead. There are creatures that prowl this forest at night that do not heed my wishes. Even I do not like to confront them. It is only a few hours until daybreak, so it will not be long." She paused. "And the Stryx have not broken through to Tartarus. Not yet." She gestured for us to follow. "Come, I will lead you to a grove where you will be safe, but you must not step outside of the boundaries until daybreak."

"All right, thank you." I struggled with my desire to charge off and stop the Stryx, but if Artemis was too afraid to confront the night creatures, I didn't want to either.

We followed Artemis through the forest. Faint moonlight filtered through the trees, turning the bark silver and the ground a dark, rich gray. Through the leaves above, I caught sight of a few stars, twinkling away. In the distance, animals rustled in the leaves, night creatures going about their business. If I focused hard enough, I could even hear their heartbeats.

"Here we are." Artemis turned and gestured to a clearing up ahead.

A beautiful blue pool sparkled under the moonlight, the color a deep rich navy in the dark. Artemis waved her hand, and a campfire burst to life next to it, warm and welcoming. Plush sleeping pads and blankets appeared next to the fire, along with trays of food and wine.

Uh-oh.

As if she could read my mind, Artemis spoke. "It is all safe for mortals to eat, I vow it. I would not give you my magic and then feed you something that might trap you in the godly realm."

I met her gaze, and believed her. "Thank you."

"When the sun rises, you may walk safely from the forest. Once you are on the outskirts, your transportation charm will work." She stepped toward me, reaching for my arm. Her touch was like lightning, but somehow, not bad. It shot power and strength through me instead of an electric current. "We believe in you, Rowan. You must believe in yourself."

Her faith in me made my eyes prickle with tears. I blinked and nodded. "Thank you."

She smiled, then turned and left, disappearing into the air as she walked.

I turned to the campfire and the picnic, my stomach already rumbling. "If you want to take the first turn in the bath, go for it." I had eyes only for the bread, cheese, and fruit laid out in front of me on beautiful golden platters.

By the time I heard splashing in the water behind me, I was already chomping away. Explosions of flavor made me swoon, and it was true—godly food is better. Everything tasted amazing. I ate and drank as Maximus bathed behind me, and it was hard not to think of what he might look like. As my hunger was sated, it became even harder to keep my mind on pure thoughts.

Maybe I should join him. That wasn't a terrible idea, was it?

"All done." His voice sounded from behind me.

Dang. Opportunity lost.

I swallowed the last bite of apple and stood, turning. His hair was damp and dark in the moonlight, and once again, I was struck by how much he looked like a fallen angel. I didn't mean to be so shallow, but it was impossible to ignore.

"Thanks." I slipped by him, headed toward the pool, and he settled by the fire to eat. I couldn't help but peek over my shoulder at him as I undressed, but he had his back politely turned.

I kind of wanted to tell him not to bother being so polite—that I might actually like it if he looked—but I couldn't figure out the words. Everything I came up with sounded awkward as hell.

Carefully, I dipped my toe into the pool, delighted to find it warm. It was about the size of my bedroom back home, and the moonlight turned the water a clear, dark midnight blue. I could just make out the big rocks that sat on the bottom.

Gratefully, I sank into the water, letting the warmth work away the soreness in my muscles. I leaned back and looked at the stars overhead, realizing that there were millions of them, all visible to the naked eye.

Delighted, I grinned. There must be no light pollution out

here. It was magical to bathe beneath the stars, beside a camp created for us by a goddess.

As the water flowed around me, I couldn't help but believe that maybe I *was* worthy. She believed in me. If freaking Artemis believed in me, maybe I needed to believe in myself.

I could do this. I'd used the magic that I'd been afraid of, proven again that I could do it. Whatever my fears were, they weren't rational. They were holdovers from my time in captivity, and I needed to remember that. It was the only way to make it through this.

Truly relaxed for the first time in months, I enjoyed my bath, stealing occasional glances at Maximus. Finished, I got out and dried myself with the white cloth sitting by the pool—really, Artemis had thought of everything—then stared at my dirty clothes in dismay.

I looked at Maximus's back. "Can you conjure me a night shirt?"

"What kind?" he asked, without turning around.

Quit being so polite and turn around, I wanted to shout. But I didn't. "Like one of your T-shirts or something."

"Sure." His magic flared briefly, then he tossed a big T-shirt over his shoulders, followed by a pair of women's underwear. They were green, and I caught them out of the air.

I held them up to inspect them, spotting the ridiculous cartoon dragon's face right on the butt. I laughed. "Nice choice."

"I thought they suited a DragonGod."

"They do indeed." I shimmied into the clothes, then joined him on the cushion near the fire.

He turned to look at me, his face highlighted by the golden glow of the fire. "You've done well here, Rowan. Artemis is right to believe in you. *I* believe in you." He hesitated a moment, and my breath caught. "I'm not very good with words, but I wanted to say..." He sucked in a deep breath. "I care for you, Rowan. You're important to me."

My heart swelled at his words. Suddenly, I was glad I hadn't shouted at him to turn around and check me out since I was naked. This was much better.

I leaned forward and pressed my lips to his, reveling in the heat of him.

"You're important to me, too," I murmured against his lips. "More important than I thought someone could be in such a short period of time."

"Fate." He pulled me to him, his lips moving expertly on mine.

There were things I wanted to say to him—words that showed how great I thought he was—but they were driven from my mind. All I could focus on was how good he felt. How his kisses made my head swoon and my body heat.

I moaned and pushed at his shoulders until he got the clue. He fell backward, and I rolled with him on the cushion until we were side by side. Then I pounced, kissing him for all I was worth.

He groaned and yanked me toward him, pressing the full length of his body against mine. Heat exploded within me, driving all rational thought from my mind.

Yes. Finally.

CHAPTER ELEVEN

I woke to the sound of the birds chirping and treetops rustling. The rising sun sent beams of light streaking through the forest, and I opened my eyes to see Maximus next to me. Memories of what we'd done flashed through my mind, heating my cheeks. Though we hadn't gone all the way, it'd easily been the best night of my life.

Quickly, before he could wake up and I started to feel awkward because I was a weirdo, I hopped up and hurried toward my pile of dirty clothes that I'd left lying by the pool. In the early morning light, the water gleamed a pale turquoise. I gave it one longing glance, then looked around for my clothes.

They were where I'd left them, folded loosely on a rock, but next to them sat a neatly folded identical pair. My heart fluttered.

Maximus must have conjured them. I tugged them on and pulled the dragon scale boat out of the pocket of my dirty jeans. I also grabbed the instructions for the spell from the Hesperides. By the time I turned toward Maximus, he was up and dressed. Man, he'd been quick and quiet.

"Morning." I could feel my cheeks go hot. Way to go, cool girl.

"Morning." His voice was warm and his smile warmer. "Ready to get going?"

"Let's get this show on the road." I grabbed my dirty clothes and approached. He conjured a backpack, then held out his hand. "I'll carry those for you."

I handed them over. "Thanks."

He shoved them in the pack, along with his dirty clothes, and slung it over his shoulder. I crouched and put together two bread and cheese sandwiches from the remains of last night's dinner, then stood and handed him one.

We set out of the forest, eating as we walked.

"Can Hedy help with the potion and spell that you need to find Atlas?" he asked.

I shook my head. "No, I don't think so. They said it was blood sorcery, and she doesn't do that. I know two people who can do it, though. Blood Sorceresses who live in Magic's Bend."

I pulled my cell phone out of my pocket and snapped a picture of the ingredient list that the Hesperides had written for me. Then I texted it to Aerdeca and Mordaca, the Blood Sorceresses that I'd met a little while ago. I didn't know them well, but for a price, they'd help me. For a price, I had a feeling they'd do just about anything.

I looked up at Maximus. "We'll see what they say."

The forest was quiet this morning, and we had no trouble from the animals. I could hear them in the distance, but they didn't bother us.

When we stepped out of the forest, I felt the crackle of the protection charm as it broke. Grass waved against my ankles, and the sun beat down strongly. My phone buzzed, and I looked down at the text message.

I read it out loud to Maximus. "We can do it tonight but we

need you to pick up an ingredient from a guy we hate. We'd do it but he sucks. Go to Blackburn Alley in Darklane and stop by The Snake Pit. Buy some hespodel from Snakerton."

"Do you know what hespodel is?" Maximus asked.

"Yes, it's a root. Pale purple with green tips. Rare and a bit expensive, but it's a great binder for more complicated spells that induce visions."

"That sounds easy enough," Maximus said. "I wonder what Snakerton's deal is?"

"Whatever it is, I bet they're right that he's a jerk. Can your transport charm take us to Magic's Bend? Near Darklane?"

"Yes." He dug into his pocket and pulled it out. "Ready?"

"As I'll ever be."

He hurled the charm to the ground, and a silvery cloud of black smoke exploded upward. I stepped in, letting the ether suck me through space and spit me out in the middle of Magic's Bend.

Given the time change, it must have been about ten at night here. The moon hung heavy in the sky, peeping out from behind a dark cloud. Drizzly rain spat from the sky, and I hunched deep into my leather jacket.

Maximus appeared next to me. "Which way?"

I pointed toward a creepy-looking street that marked the entrance to Darklane, the part of town where dark magic practitioners lived. The residents weren't all evil, but many of them could be. Darklane was where you lived and worked if you didn't want the law looking too closely into your activities. Some types of magic—like the blood magic that Aerdeca and Mordaca practiced—weren't explicitly evil. It was all about context. If the blood was voluntarily given, it was fine. If not, well, then obviously it was bad business.

"Come on. Let's go find this Snakerton dude." I walked toward the main street that cut through Darklane. The air was somehow heavier here, more difficult to breathe. The modern street turned to cobblestones in that part of town, a remnant of the past from a neighborhood that refused to change.

We stepped into the watery golden light that gleamed from the gas lamps and started down the sidewalk. The buildings were all three-story Victorian houses. Long ago, the colorful exteriors had been covered by a soot-like substance, residue of the dark magic that gave this place its name.

Shadowy alleys stretched away into the distance, and I skirted around them.

I squinted into the distance, looking for the street sign for Blackburn Alley. The rain made it a bit hard to see, so I tried harder. Finally, I spotted it and pointed. "There it is."

"You can read that?"

"Yeah, you can't?"

"I have twenty-twenty vision, and no, I can't."

"Ah, cool. The animals in Artemis's forest gave me superior hearing, and they must have given me better vision as well." It wasn't something I'd noticed right away, because I hadn't tried using it. But now that I'd tried...well, that was damned cool.

We hurried to the road and took a left turn onto it. The road was more of an alley than anything else, the narrow cobblestone street uneven in places. It was only about six feet wide, and the buildings loomed on either side, their second and third floors hanging out farther than the ones below. It gave the street a tunnel-like feel.

The whole place reeked of dark magic, and the stuff in the shop windows made me shiver. Weird weapons that looked more like torture devices, potions that glittered with an evil hue, and shrunken heads—*real* shrunken heads—were all for sale.

The rain began to fall harder as we walked, gleaming on the cobblestones beneath our feet. By the time we saw the sign for The Snake Pit, I was chilled to the bone.

Fortunately, it was still open even at this late hour. Though in fairness, most businesses in Darklane were probably more active late at night.

The door creaked as Maximus opened it, and I slipped into the smoky interior. A purple haze filled the space that reeked of herbs. My nose wrinkled as my eyes watered. It was a cluttered little place, with shelves stocked full of ratty old books and vials of stuff that I didn't want to explore too closely. Most of it appeared to be related to potion making, however, and that piqued my interest.

"Can I help you?" The pompous voice came from the back, and I peeked around a shelf to get a look at the speaker.

He was younger than I expected, mid-thirties at the oldest. Slim and short, his hair was done up in a series of complicated waves. He had the curled mustache of a cartoon villain, and I seriously expected him to start yelling at some meddlesome kids.

And the cologne...

Oh fates, the cologne. It nearly choked me.

Carefully, I breathed through my mouth and said, "We're here to buy some hespodel."

He grinned widely. "What a wise and beautiful woman, to request hespodel. You must be very talented with potions."

I frowned, trying hard not to give him the stink eye. But seriously, what was up with the excessive flattery that came out of the blue? Was he trying for manipulation? If so, it was ridiculously transparent.

"Yep. That's me. Extremely wise and beautiful." I smiled, trying not to show too many teeth in case it looked like a grimace or a snarl. Honestly, either would have suited my mood, but neither would get me what I wanted. "So, the hespodel?"

"Yes, yes, just a moment." He disappeared behind some cluttered shelves. A rattling noise followed. He came out with a little box made of semitransparent gray glass. Within, there was a stalk of hespodel.

He handed it to me. "An intelligent woman such as yourself will see that everything is in order. I'd love to see what amazing concoction you whip up with that."

Okay, weirdo. I took the box and squinted hard at the hespodel, trying to see through the milky gray glass. It didn't look quite right. I opened the little box to inspect it closer.

Yep. That plant was a medium tone purple, not pale purple. And were those tips painted on?

I scowled, then looked up at Snakerton. "This isn't hespodel."

He put on a confused expression and looked down at the box. "But of course it is!"

"I know my hespodel, and that's not it. The colors are wrong." And I'd bet twenty bucks that his dumb flattery was an attempt to distract me from noticing that he was shady. I hated manipulators.

Too bad for him, he was terrible at it.

"Do you have real hespodel?" Maximus asked, his voice sharp.

Snakerton jumped slightly, then looked up at Maximus, who loomed over him. His expression turned sour. "I must have made a mistake. Let me check."

He repeated the procedure with going behind the shelves and making a bit of noise. The compliments started flowing before he'd even reappeared. The dude couldn't seem to help himself.

"In your esteemed wisdom, I'm sure you'll see that this is the proper variety of hespodel." He walked around from behind the shelving and handed me another box.

Even before I opened the box, I knew it wasn't hespodel. I checked anyway. The plant was too curvy. I snapped the box shut and looked at Snakerton. "Why are you giving me the wrong plant?"

"Wh-what?" he sputtered. "I'm not!"

Maximus stepped forward, looking even bigger when he was up close to the little snake. I'd have tried intimidating Snakerton myself, but I could already tell he was the kind of guy who respected men more. Maximus was the right choice for this particular job.

"Why?" Maximus asked. "Answer her question."

Snakerton alternately turned white and red, going from fear to anger and back again. "I'm just trying to get ahead, okay? The world is an ugly place, and I'm just doing what I can to make it."

"By cheating people?" I asked. That was what he'd been trying to do. Pass some cheap stuff off as the expensive stuff and charge me more for nothing.

He shrugged. "So what? *People* aren't me, so they don't matter."

My brows rose. "Straight to the point. And boldly said."

He leered at me. "I'm a bold man."

"Oh, dude, putting it on a little thick," I said.

Maximus gave him a condescending stare.

He deflated.

"Seriously," I said. "Do you have hespodel? I'll buy it if you have it, but I'm not giving you that much money for an inferior product."

He got a calculating look in his eye. "I do have it. But now I don't know if I want to sell it to you."

"Because I didn't play your little game?"

He sulked. Man, this guy was a piece of work.

"What do you want for the hespodel?" Maximus asked. "Sell it to us, and we'll leave you alone."

"You really want it, huh?" A cunning gleam entered Snakerton's beady eyes. "Well, then. You'll have to fight me for it."

"Fight you?" Maximus looked him up and down. "You're sure that's the way you'd like to go?"

"Not a physical fight, you Neanderthal." Snakerton puffed up his chest. "But I could take you if I wanted."

Maximus didn't bother replying.

"We could just search your shop and take it," I said. "It's not my normal style, but we're desperate."

"You'd steal from me?" His brows rose.

"No, we'd leave money on the counter." It was actually not the worst idea. We could pay double to try to make up for it. I stepped toward the back of the shop, and my foot stopped in midair.

Snakerton grinned, his expression slimy. "You can't steal from here. My shop is protected against it."

"We'd leave money," I said. "Double. And I mean it."

He shrugged. "I don't care. And the charms on the shop don't care, either. They know you're going to take it without my consent."

I tried to move my foot again, but it was stuck solid. Damn, these were some good protection charms. "What do you want, then? It really is an emergency."

Snakerton mulled it over, tapping his chin. "We'll have a friendly little competition. Me and the lady here. She clearly knows her stuff. I know my stuff. We'll each try to make a potion that is meant to levitate a heavy object. If hers can make a heavier object float high off the ground, then she can buy the hespodel. If I win, then she gives me the money for the hespodel but leaves empty-handed."

Tricky bastard. Levitation potions were quick to make, but they were tough. Like, really tough. And he thought I wasn't up to it.

I grinned. "Show me the hespodel first."

He looked offended. "You don't trust my word?"

I just laughed.

He harrumphed and went to the back of the shop, then returned very shortly with another box. A quick glance showed that it actually was hespodel. A little dried out and old, but it should still do the trick.

"Fine." I held up the box. "But I want to put this outside of the protection charm, just in case you go back on your word."

He scowled, clearly offended.

I held my ground, glaring.

"Fine." He pointed to the door. "Put it in the planter out front. No one will bother it this time of night. No one will even see it."

I hurried out the door and onto the stoop, spotting the planter immediately. It held some spikey black plants, and I stuck the little box behind it where it was well hidden.

I returned, dusting off my hands. "Let's make this quick."

"You can use anything in the shop."

"Sure thing." I moved away from him, quickly grabbing vials and ingredients. Thank fates I'd been practicing my potions so much to make up for my lack of magic.

I might have magic now, but this was still coming in handy. I made a point to mix the potion behind a bookcase where he couldn't see me, primarily because I didn't want him spotting my secret ingredient. A splash of healing potion from my utility belt. It was a little secret I'd picked up in a dusty old book in the library. A splash of highly concentrated healing draft could enhance the power of most potions.

When I was done, I brought the little bowl of liquid out from behind my counter. Snakerton was still busily mixing away. He'd put on some funny little goggles and was moving his wrists with serious flair.

Overkill.

"Almost done?" I asked.

He looked up and glared. "That was fast."

"Come on, I bet you can keep up."

"Keep up? Keep up!" he sputtered.

"So that means you're done with your potion?"

He mixed it again with one quick flick of his wrist. "Yes!"

I gestured to his potion. "Gentlemen first, then."

"But it's ladies first."

"We don't need to stand on ceremony, do we, pal?"

He thought for a moment, then shrugged, picked up his bowl of potion, and walked to a bookshelf that stood chest high. It was the second largest piece of furniture in the room. "I will lift this bookshelf. It weighs at least a thousand pounds."

He poured his potion on top of the bookshelf. Magic sparked in the air, and the thing began to levitate, lifting two feet off the ground. I glanced at Maximus, who watched intently. He didn't look impressed.

Snakerton thrust out his hands in a gesture of carnival showmanship. "Beat that!"

"No problem." I pointed to the biggest bookshelf in the place. It was twice as tall as the one he'd lifted and stuffed full of heavy books. Since it was the only thing bigger in the room, I'd have to try to lift it if I wanted to win. "How heavy do you think that is?"

"At least three thousand pounds." He scoffed. "But you can't lift that."

"Sure I can." I poured some of my potion onto an empty shelf. The whole thing began to levitate, but it stopped abruptly only an inch off the ground.

"See!" he crowed. "I told you!"

"It levitated," I said. But not as high as I'd expected. Which was weird.

"Not high enough," he said.

"We didn't establish those rules," I said. "It just had to levitate. You can't change the rules partway through so that you get what you want." But why didn't it go higher? It really should have gone higher.

Maximus crouched low on the ground and peered under the shelves. He made a disgusted noise and stood. "Cheater."

"What?" I crouched low and checked. There was a hollow space in the bottom of the shelf. At each of the four corners, a heavy chain connected the bookshelf to the floor. I looked up at Snakerton, disgusted. "It's not even clever. You should have made the chains invisible."

His jaw dropped.

I drew my electric sword from the ether and sliced through each of the chains. The bookshelf floated higher.

I stood, grinning. "There, I officially win. Now give me the hespodel."

He glared. "Fine. You owe me eighty-five dollars."

I really didn't want to pay this dick, not after the trick he'd pulled. After cheating, he didn't deserve it. But I wanted to get out of here without a fight, so I pulled a wad of cash from my pocket and walked toward the door. He followed.

I stepped outside and retrieved the hespodel, making sure it was still the proper ingredient and that a trick hadn't been pulled. It looked fine. I gave him the bills.

Quickly, he fanned through them, then squawked. "There's only sixty here!"

"Yeah, I docked your pay for cheating." I grinned. "See you later, Snakerton."

We walked out into the rain.

"Nice work," Maximus said.

"Thanks. I hate it when cheaters like him win."

"Don't we all."

Together, we hurried out of Blackburn Alley and onto the main street. The rain had lightened to a drizzle by the time we approached the Apothecary's Jungle where Aerdeca and Mordaca lived and worked. I climbed the narrow stairs as the sign over our heads swung and creaked in the wind.

Quickly, I knocked on a door that had probably once been purple but was so thickly covered in dark magic residue that it was hard to tell.

Beneath my hand, the door creaked open.

I looked at Maximus. "That's weird."

"They normally open it themselves?"

"I don't know. I've only been here once. But yeah, I would think they'd normally open it themselves. They've got a lot of valuable stuff in here. Plus, they live here." I turned back to the door and squinted through the gap. All I could make out was a dark foyer with cobwebs in the ceiling.

Then a scream tore through the house.

CHAPTER TWELVE

My heart leapt into my chest at the sound of the scream, and I sprinted into the foyer, skidding on the black and white tiles. The ornate black velvet wallpaper sucked up all the light from the dusty old chandelier, and I had to squint to find an exit.

The scream sounded again, one of rage rather than terror.

"It's coming from that way." Maximus pointed to a narrow hall that led off of the foyer.

We sprinted down the hall, past old oil portraits that seemed to watch us.

Another scream. Then another.

I rushed into an ornate living room just in time to see Aerdeca and Mordaca throw a bucket of gray water on a poltergeist. The creature looked enraged, its transparent face twisted in a snarl. When the water hit it, the beast hissed and disappeared, driven off by whatever was in the potion.

Aerdeca and Mordaca stood in the middle of the living room, panting.

"Glad I got here in time to help," I said.

They turned, each wearing their signature outfit. Mordaca's midnight hair was done up in a bouffant, rising high toward the ceiling. It matched her slinky black dress that revealed so much cleavage she could probably rest her chin on her boobs if she tried. Okay, exaggeration. But not by much.

The black tips on her nails and the heavy black makeup around her eyes completed the look. Elvira-chic, I liked to think of it. She smiled a wicked smile, her red lips parting to reveal white teeth that might as well have been fangs.

Aerdeca was her opposite, in a sleek white pantsuit with blonde hair that flowed like water over her shoulders. Her makeup was natural and her expression serene. Nude polish on her nails would have looked like something on the girl next door, except that they were filed into vicious points. All in all, she looked cool as hell.

The uninitiated might think that Aerdeca was the nice one because she wore white and had a sweeter voice.

They'd be wrong.

Neither of them was nice.

But you could count on them to do what you paid them for. And in a pinch, they'd have your back. I'd heard whispered rumors of them in battles, fighting on the side of right, but hadn't seen it myself.

"I thought you specialized in potions," I said. "Not poltergeists."

Mordaca got a slightly shifty look in her eyes, which surprised me.

"Of course we do." Her voice was whiskey-rough and low.

"Just a little trouble with an unwanted guest," Aerdeca said.

Hmmm. From the glance they shared with each other, there was more to the story. But no way I'd press for it.

Their secrets were their secrets, after all. Just like mine were mine.

I held up the little box. "I got the hespodel." I hiked a thumb toward Maximus. "And this is my friend Maximus. Maximus, this is Aerdeca and Mordaca."

"Delighted, friend." Aerdeca's brows rose appreciatively. She gave him the up and down and wasn't subtle about it.

"Keep it in your pants," I said.

She just laughed.

"Let's get this show on the road," Mordaca said. "I have a party to get to."

"This late?" I asked. It had to be near midnight.

"The day has just started, honey." Mordaca grinned.

"Don't listen to her," Aerdeca said. "It's past my bedtime. We need to get this over with."

I followed them through the living room, which looked a bit like a fancy gothic funeral parlor.

Their workshop was different, though. Lighter, with a big wooden table in the middle and shelves on the wall that were stuffed full of potion-making supplies. An enormous hearth burned away at one end, and dried herbs hung from the ceiling.

Aerdeca and Mordaca turned to me.

"That'll be three grand," Mordaca said.

I winced. "Do you take card?"

Fates, how long would this take me to pay off?

Maximus was quick, though, handing them his card.

"You don't have to do that," I said.

"This isn't a date. We're saving the world." He smiled down at me. "But I would like to take you on a date eventually. After the world has been saved."

I grinned stupidly, and I swore to god I heard Mordaca sigh. It sounded like a noise a high school girl would make, and was so out of character that I goggled at her.

She shrugged a shoulder clad in black satin. "What? I'm a romantic."

"And I'm a businesswoman." Aerdeca swiped the card

through a little machine. It beeped a few times, then she handed the card back.

Mordaca rubbed her hands together. "Let's do this."

"Can I see the original instructions?" Aerdeca asked. "I hate working off a phone."

I dug into my pocket and handed them to her, then set the box of hespodel on the table.

Mordaca joined Aerdeca, and they both bent over the piece of paper, reading quietly. Occasionally they'd jostle each other and someone would get an elbow in the side, but eventually they looked up.

"This won't take long, but it might not be fun," Mordaca said.

"What do you mean, not fun?" Maximus asked. "Dangerous?"

Aerdeca shrugged, clearly unconcerned. "Maybe. This stuff usually is. And this spell? Well, it's a tricky one."

"What does it involve?" I'd read it but had only understood the potion bit. I didn't get the rest of it.

"The goal is to induce a trance that will show you where to go to find Atlas," Mordaca said. "But it can be, ah, stressful to the body."

"It'll hurt like hell." Aerdeca didn't sugarcoat it.

"I'll do it, then," Maximus said.

I grabbed his arm. "No. It has to be me."

"No, it doesn't."

"This is part of my journey as a DragonGod. Anyway, it might help that I'm the Greek DragonGod and I'm seeking a Greek titan."

"She has a point," Mordaca said. "I do think that her connection to Atlas will make it more effective."

Maximus frowned. "More effective? So it would still be mostly effective if I did it?"

"We can't risk it." I squeezed his arm. "We need to find him.

There's too much at stake. But thank you for wanting to do it so I don't have to."

He looked at me, his gaze intense. "Always."

I wanted to kiss him, but was one hundred percent sure that would get us a whistle from Mordaca.

I turned to them. "Okay, let's do this."

"You can sit in front of the fire." Aerdeca dragged a heavy wooden chair and positioned it in front of the flickering flames. Orange and red danced within the hearth, along with hints of white and blue.

I did as she commanded, letting the heat warm me. They began to bustle around the room behind me, and I turned to watch them combine various ingredients in a bowl. The last addition was the hespodel, which they dropped in without cutting up. The bowl smoked and fizzed.

Mordaca picked it up, while Aerdeca grabbed a long silver blade. I swallowed hard.

They approached, the firelight glinting eerily on their faces.

"Raise your hand," Aerdeca said.

I did as she asked.

Mordaca held the bowl under my hand, while Aerdeca sliced the knife across my fingertip. Pain flared.

"As you bleed, think of your intentions toward Atlas. Really focus on it," Aerdeca said.

I closed my eyes and imagined meeting him and asking him how to stop the Stryx and heal the Amazons and himself. It was easy to play it out in my mind, and I wondered if someone could fake this process. Probably not.

"That's enough." Aerdeca handed me a small white cloth, and I pressed it to my fingertip.

Mordaca withdrew the bowl and took it back to the table. I turned to watch her and Aerdeca stand over it, their hands outstretched to hover over the top. Light flashed at their palms, and they began to chant.

Magic filled the air, rolling over me. It brought with it the burn of whiskey from Mordaca and the sound of birds from Aerdeca. The liquid in the bowl bubbled up to the surface, smoking violently.

The chanting stopped abruptly, and the smoke died down. The scent of lavender filled the room.

"Looks like it worked," Aerdeca said.

"Now for the shitty part." Mordaca picked up the bowl and walked toward me.

"You really know how to put a girl at ease, Mordaca."

She grinned widely, her red lips glinting in the firelight like fresh blood. "What can I say? I'm a people pleaser."

"Surrre."

She handed me the bowl. "Drink most of it, then toss a bit in the fire. Whatever vision you see afterward is where you're supposed to go to find Atlas. So try to remember it all. Pick up any details you can."

I nodded, then tentatively sniffed the liquid. Still smelled like lavender. Not so bad.

I raised the bowl to my mouth and gulped.

Ugh.

Tasted of old fish. I nearly gagged, but forced myself to swallow the majority of the potion. Sweat popped out at my temples from the nausea roiling within me. I leaned forward and tossed the last bit of the liquid into the fire, then handed the bowl to Mordaca.

"So, when will these visions st—"

The fire flamed high, and I snapped my mouth shut. It blasted forward, enveloping me. Pain streaked through me as the heat snapped at my skin.

"You're not really burning!" Mordaca's words filtered through the agony that made me want to curl up in a ball and die. "Don't be afraid."

Afraid?

I could barely process her words, it hurt so bad. I tried to scream, but the noise was trapped in my throat. I was frozen solid, unable to move. Agony like I'd never known tore through my whole body.

"Stop this!" Maximus's voice broke through the pain. "She's screaming. This can't be right."

"She's fine. Shut up!" Aerdeca's voice cracked like a whip, though I couldn't see her. All I could see was the flame. "Let her finish. She needs to see where Atlas is."

Atlas.

I clung to the name like a lifeline. The agony still tore through me, but I had to focus. They said this would suck; I'd known that going in.

Every muscle in my body ached and my skin felt like it'd melted off, but I tried to push it from my mind, focusing only on thoughts of Atlas.

I have to find you. I have to save you.

A vision blasted into my mind, a mountain range soaring toward the sky. An ancient Greek ruin sat at the top, marble columns and blocks scattered across the mountaintop—the remains of a once great temple.

Seek the Oracle at Delphi. The words resounded through my mind, and I imprinted them in my memory. I used the pain as fuel, determined to get something out of this misery.

The fire faded away, and I sagged, flopping to the floor like a dead fish. Though the heat was gone, every muscle in my body was on fire from going rigid during the worst of the pain.

Maximus fell to his knees at my side, his face so white I thought he might pass out. His eyes were stark, pupils blown out. "Are you all right?" His voice was rough when he spoke, as if he'd been shouting.

"Fine." I blinked, trying to clear my blurry vision as I sat. The movement took everything I had, and by the time I was sitting upright, I was sweating.

Maximus supported me. "What can I get you?"

Mordaca knelt in front of me, her black dress pooling on the ground. She thrust a cup at me. "Here, drink this. It will make you feel better."

Maximus nearly snarled at her. "What's in it?"

"A restorative potion."

I grabbed it, not the least bit concerned. Maximus might have trust issues with Mordaca, but I'd asked for that misery. Insisted on it, in fact. I felt like a bit of a moron now, but it'd had to be done.

I raised the glass and sucked down the liquid, which didn't taste like dead fish, thank fates. There was a nice hint of grapefruit and rosemary, and as the potion filled my belly, warmth and strength rushed through my limbs.

It felt a bit like sucking the life out of plants. Though I was grateful to get the benefit without actually having to do the plant murdering.

I drank the last sip and lowered the cup. "I know where to go."

Mordaca and Aerdeca leaned forward, their eyes bright. "Where?"

"Delphi. We have to see the Oracle."

Aerdeca's brows rose. She was clearly impressed. "Wow. She's quite famous. Been dead a while, though, I thought."

"A couple thousand years, at least," Mordaca said. "But that won't stop a proper Oracle. You'll have to let us know what she's like."

I nodded and started to stand. Maximus was quicker, rising

to his feet and pulling me up. I smiled up at him, trying to look healthy and hale. "Seriously, I'm fine."

"You didn't look fine."

"That was then; this is now. And we've got to get to Greece."

As it turned out, the best way to get to Delphi was by motorcycle. There was the Delphi that the humans knew of, the place that was frequently flooded with tour busses and cameras. But the *real* Delphi—the one with the Oracle and the biggest temples— was located on another mountain, far from the prying eyes of humans. None of them had ever seen it, in fact.

Fortunately, Maximus had a friend in the area. Axios the cheetah shifter had hooked us up with two motorcycles and directed us to the remote mountain road that led up to the real Delphi.

It was a sunny afternoon in Greece. I couldn't believe it was the same day that we'd departed the forest. Wind whipped through my hair as we took the curves at sharp angles, speeding up into the mountains. I'd never ridden a motorcycle before, but it turned out I was a natural.

I pressed on the gas and sped ahead of Maximus.

"Be careful!" His voice was a whisper behind me, drowned out by the engine and the wind and my sheer joy in the ride.

When I crested the hill and spotted Delphi on the next ridge over, I grinned. It looked just as it had in my vision. Dozens of white columns speared the sky, surrounded by thousands of massive marble blocks that had once made up the many buildings at the sacred site. Most of those buildings were in pieces now, but there were a few left standing.

It didn't take long to reach the main gate, which soared high, white marble against blue sky. I stopped my bike and stared at it.

Maximus did the same, his brow furrowed as he inspected the marble gate.

There was no door, just an archway of marble, but it sure felt like something guarded it.

"There's something off," Maximus said. "We shouldn't just walk through. There's something tricky about this."

"Agreed." I eyed the gate, feeling the protective magic prickle toward me. I wasn't sure what would go wrong if I entered without an invitation, but I was pretty sure I didn't want to find out.

To the right of the gate was a flat marble slab. A sculpture of a man loomed over it. He carried a lyre and wore a wreath around his head. At his feet, there were a few bundles of dead flowers, a couple candles, and a few coins. I pursed my lips.

"That's got to be Apollo," I said. "I read that this city was kind of like *his* city. The temples were named after him and all that. So maybe we have to make an offering to him."

Maximus nodded. "The Romans were really into this sort of thing. Probably took it right from the Greeks."

"What do you suggest as an offering?"

"Money often does the trick." He pointed to the bouquets. "Some flowers. Something that is valuable monetarily and personally is good, too."

"Like a weapon," I said.

"That'd be good." He climbed off his motorcycle, and magic crackled briefly as he pulled a sword from the ether. It was finely crafted, with a beautiful hilt and a wicked edge. "I've always liked this one."

He laid it on the stone in front of Apollo's feet. I followed suit, conjuring one of my favorite daggers. The hilt had two little onyx stones inset into the head of a dragon. A bit of a personal joke, really, since I was supposed to be a dragon.

I put the dagger at Apollo's feet.

The air changed immediately. Now that we'd both made a sacrifice, the protection charm on the archway disappeared.

"That did it." Maximus strode through.

I followed, feeling no change in the air.

The ruins were completely silent. Even the birds weren't singing in here. Only the wind moved, blowing gently through the space that possessed the kind of heaviness that I associated with ancient places.

Slowly, we walked up a central lane. Huge stone buildings had collapsed on either side. Here and there, statues peeked up, somehow still standing after years of neglect.

As we passed one of a huge warrior, magic prickled on the air. The statue held his shield and sword in front of him, ready to fight.

I shifted to look at him as we walked by, and magic surged from him. He leapt off his marble pedestal, and my heart jumped.

"Attack!" I shouted the warning to Maximus as I drew my shield and electric sword from the ether.

The marble warrior charged, swinging his blade. I raised my shield, and his sword crashed into it. My arm shook from the blow as I pivoted and swiped out with my blade, hitting him in the shoulder. It didn't make a dent, and I danced backward.

Out of the corner of my eye, I caught sight of Maximus fighting another statue. This one was even bigger than mine.

I turned my attention toward my attacker, feinting left and then going right, striking with my blade. It bounced off him again, and whatever magic protected him was strong.

His stone sword glanced off my arm, making pain flare. I stumbled backward.

Behind me, Maximus swung his sword with such force that the statue shattered into a dozen pieces. I'd landed several blows, but these guys apparently could only be defeated with godly strength.

The statue lunged toward me, swinging his blade. I dodged another blow, bringing my own sword up and slicing toward his arm. I gave it my all, but my sword made no dent. I felt the reverberations of the strike all the way up my arm, and winced.

"I've got this," Maximus said from behind.

I darted left, clearing the path for him. He charged, all grace and fury. With one swipe to the warrior's waist, he shattered the statue.

Panting, I spun in a circle, inspecting our surroundings. No other statues came alive.

"Holy fates, what was that all about?" I asked.

"Perhaps they protect the Oracle." Maximus spun in a circle as well, checking out the territory.

"Let's go, then, before any more come alive."

We passed by a huge temple to Apollo that was still almost entirely intact, but I shook my head. "I don't think the Oracle is in there. In my vision, there was a small round building with a domed roof."

We kept going, passing by an amphitheater built into the cliff and a circular area made of dozens of columns.

"Is that it?" Maximus pointed to the right.

I turned, catching sight of a little round building. I smiled. "Yeah, that's it."

We hurried toward it, climbing over rocks and fallen columns, until we finally reached the entrance.

"It looks like it was built yesterday." Awed, I ran my hands over the smooth stone of the exterior wall.

"People take care of it. Look here." Maximus pointed to a deep crack in one of the stones that had been carefully mended. "The place isn't really used anymore, but whoever lives nearby hasn't let the temple to Apollo fall into ruin. Or the Oracle's chambers."

"Faith and knowledge, the two things people care about most."

"And sports."

I grinned, looking at him. "Fond of football, are you?"

"Not particularly. But if there's one thing I've noticed about modern day, sports are even more of a religion now than they used to be. If this place had had a football field, it'd be in perfect condition, I guarantee it."

I chuckled. "Ready to go in?"

He sucked in a breath. "Let's meet the Oracle."

Side by side, we stepped into the cool, quiet space. The only light came from the doorway, so it was pretty dark. I squinted, making out a round room that was entirely empty. The only interesting feature in the whole place was the deep chasm in the floor. Steam wafted up from it, smelling faintly sweet.

"Hello? Oracle?" I asked. "We're looking for Atlas. We were told you could help us find him."

"Begone, intruders!" The voice bellowed through the small space, bouncing off the walls and seeming to grow louder on the echo. "Begone, or I shall smite you!"

I winced, my ears ringing from the Oracle's shouts. "We can't leave. We need help."

"Begone!"

"Should we make an offering?" Maximus asked.

I nodded. "Couldn't hurt. Should we throw it in the chasm, do you think?"

"Throw it in my chasm!" the Oracle screeched. This time, she sounded female. And pissed off. "Don't you dare throw garbage in my chasm."

Okay, that was an odd choice of words. "We won't! Will you come out and help us?"

"Will it make you leave me alone? And not attack my statues on the way out?"

"Definitely," I said.

"Fine," the Oracle grumbled.

In front of us, the air shimmered with a blue sheen. It grew darker and darker as a figure coalesced from the mist that rose up from the chasm. She was indeed female, and looked to be roughly eight hundred years old. She wore a velour track suit and sat in a ghostly armchair.

She scowled at us, her eyes bright. "You're interrupting my stories. Now, what do you want?"

"You watch soaps?" I wouldn't have pegged the ancient Oracle for a soap watcher.

"Of course I watch my stories. Who doesn't watch the soaps?"

"I do, of course," Maximus said. "I'm particular to *All My Children*."

"That's been off the air for years!"

"Older episodes, of course." He delivered the line so smoothly that I bought it. And hey, maybe he did watch soaps, though I doubted it. Not much time for TV when you were pulling double duty at the Order and the Protectorate.

The Oracle grumbled. "I suppose it was fine, but I'm really more interested in *General Hospital*."

"That's a good one, too." The corner of Maximus's lip crept up, as if he were trying not to laugh. His shoulders convulsed just slightly.

Oh, shit. He *was* trying not to laugh.

"So, Oracle," I said, hoping to distract her from the fact that Maximus definitely had no idea what he was talking about and that his charade was collapsing. "We were hoping you could tell us about Atlas. We want to help him, but we can't find him."

She shook her head. "Paranoid ninny, with his bolt holes and hidey holes and all the rest of it. Those gods sure did a number on him."

"It sounds like the titans got a really raw deal," I said.

"No, they didn't do well after the war. Atlas and Prometheus were the lucky ones. The rest of the poor bastards ended up in Tartarus." She settled back, getting comfy. "Now, don't get me wrong. A more murderous and dangerous bunch of evil giants I've never met. They should be locked up. But Prometheus and Atlas weren't so bad."

"Can you help us find him?" Maximus said. "We think he's sick. We need to help him, like Dr. Quartermaine would do."

"*Now* you're speaking my language." She got a dreamy cast to her eyes. "Ah, that Dr. Quartermaine."

I waited a moment to see if she would finish her thought, but she just kept staring off into space, looking relaxed and happy. Hmmmm.

"We'd like to help Atlas," I reminded her.

She snapped to attention. "Yes, yes. Of course. You will find a portal to his domain here, in Delphi. It is the circle of columns that you passed on your way to my chambers. If you enter it and say the name Atlas three times in a row, the portal will activate and take you to his fortress."

"Thank you."

Maximus smiled at her. "Enjoy your stories."

"I will, dearie. You too."

With that, we left the famous Oracle at Delphi and walked back out into the sun. As we headed toward the portal to Atlas's domain, I peered up at Maximus. "Dr. Quartermaine?"

"*General Hospital.* Though honestly, I was just throwing out TV names and hoping something hit."

"Really?"

"While I was learning about the modern world, I watched a lot of TV to figure things out." He scrubbed a hand over his face.

"Though for a while there, I thought modern people were insane. So much coming back from the dead and secret babies."

"Yeah, they play that up a bit in the soaps." I stopped in front of the circle.

Twenty columns reached toward the sky, each positioned to form a perfect circle. I reached for Maximus's hand. He gripped mine.

Together, we stepped inside the circle and let the ether sweep us away.

CHAPTER THIRTEEN

The ether pulled us through space, making my head spin. When I arrived on the other side, I blinked, taking in my surroundings. We were still in the mountains, but it was *weird.*

There were enormous protrusions of rock sticking straight out of the earth, and one of them was wide enough to hold a fortress at the very top. The walls were perfectly vertical—it'd be nearly impossible to get in.

I groaned. "Fantastic."

"It's an excellent fortress. I have to give him that."

"What do you want to bet we have to climb up?"

"I'm afraid I can't take that bet. Atlas doesn't seem like the sort of man to make things easy."

"Nope." I started toward the massive rock with the fortress on top. It was a few hundred yards away, and we had to pick our way over the hilly ground studded with rocks. The fortress looked silent and still. Not a single person to be seen on the high walls, not a sound to be heard. The setting sun gleamed on the pale rock, making it look more like a statue than a real place.

My comms charm buzzed around my neck. "Rowan? Are you there?" Ana whispered.

"I'm here. I can talk."

"How's it coming?"

"We think we might have found Atlas. We may be close to an answer about how to stop this."

"Good. Because we have a problem. Cell phones have started to go out all over the world. GPS is having problems. We think the satellites are failing. We don't have long before the military loses their connections, and war will start soon after."

Shit.

It was Atlas's job to keep the magic in space from screwing with that stuff. Did that mean he was dead?

Oh fates, please no.

"We'll hurry," I said. "Any luck with breaking through the barrier?"

"No, but Hedy has developed a bomb that can take out the entire barrier if we can get it inside the dome."

"You can't just throw it in?"

"It bounces off the boundary."

"I could take it in. I'm the only one who can get past the barrier."

"No, it will detonate soon after it leaves the power source. You'd die with it. Anyway, as long as the Stryx can call you to them, it's too dangerous."

"Okay, yeah, that's a bad plan, then. I'll see what I can figure out about the barrier and the Stryx. It'll be soon, I promise. I'll figure this out."

"Stay safe," she said.

"You too. Love you."

"Love you." She cut the line.

I looked at Maximus. "I hope we're not too late."

"We aren't."

"How do you know?"

He shrugged. "Honestly, I don't. But I'd rather assume we're not."

"Sounds good to me." We reached the base of the rock, and I tilted my head back, staring straight up. "It's got to be at least three hundred meters to the top."

Magic swelled around Maximus, and he conjured some modern climbing equipment. He handed me a harness, along with a length of rope and a bag full of something that sounded like metal bits.

He grinned. "Safety first."

I peered in the bag, spotting a bunch of metal spike-like things and a hammer.

"Put on the harness and attach the rope to it. Every twenty feet, pound in an anchor and attach your rope to it. If you fall, you're less likely to die."

"Less likely to die." I nodded. "Now you're speaking my language."

I put the harness on, and he helped me hook up the ropes.

Together, we began to climb. It was easy going at first, the slope more gradual near the bottom. I fumbled the first metal pin I tried to pound into a crevice in the rock, but got the hang of it eventually.

As we ascended, the wall became steeper, turning nearly vertical within about sixty feet. My muscles started to burn and my fingertips tingled.

"You've got it," Maximus said.

He didn't sound or look the least bit out of breath, and I'd have assumed he was a professional mountain climber.

About halfway up, I peeked down and nearly hurled. I'd never considered myself to be someone afraid of heights, but the world looked so far away from up here. The protection of the rope and metal pins seemed iffy when they were the only thing between me and certain death.

I sucked in a deep breath and looked upward.

Don't think about it.

Hand over hand, I climbed. I focused only on the immediate task ahead of me. Climb. Find a handhold. Pound in the pin. Clip off the rope. Repeat.

By the time we reached the bottom of the fortress wall, sweat was dripping down my back.

"The fortress wall is too smooth to climb," Maximus said.

"Atlas! Hey, Atlas!" I shouted. "We're here to help you, but is there a door to this thing?"

There was only silence.

Damn.

I looked at Maximus. "What do you suggest?"

His magic sparked on the air again, smelling of cedar and sounding like the roar of a waterfall. A moment later, he held a weird-looking gun in one hand. A grappling hook and line protruded from the front.

"Nice." I watched as he leaned far back and shot the thing toward the upper wall. It looked hard to get a good angle, but he caught the wall. "Where'd you learn all this stuff?"

"Did some time with a mercenary band when I first arrived in this century. Didn't like the work they did, but I learned some stuff." He yanked on the rope, testing it. "Let me go first. Once I'm at the top, I'll secure it. Then you climb up."

"What if it's not already secure and you fall?"

He thought for a moment, then conjured another grappling hook gun and set it on a tiny ledge next to him. "Hopefully my harness will catch me, though I'll be falling from pretty far. If I don't make it, try again with this grappling hook."

I scowled. "That's a shit plan. You're still dead at the end of it."

"I think it will work. Trust me." He grabbed the line trailing down from the hook and began to climb, his feet propped on the smooth fortress wall.

My heart lodged in my throat as I watched him. He was quick and graceful, but it didn't make it any easier to wait while he risked his life.

Finally, he reached the top and swung a leg over. I listened keenly for any sound of an intruder alarm going off, but my new animal senses picked up nothing.

A moment later, he leaned over the ledge and called down, "Your turn."

I nodded and grabbed the line, climbing as quickly as I could. My hands were sweaty, but I made it. Barely. By the time I swung my leg over the edge, I was tingling and light-headed.

My feet solid on the ramparts, I turned to Maximus. "Looks like I'm afraid of heights."

"You did great."

I smiled, then turned to check out the eerily quiet fortress. We stood on a wall that surrounded an open courtyard full of buildings. There were no signs of life—no plants or animals or people—and the buildings looked like they'd been abandoned for years.

"No one is here."

"Let's look around." He pointed to our left. "There are some stairs."

We hurried to the stairs and descended as quietly as we could. When we got to the bottom of the courtyard, I tilted my head, listening. "Hang on, I think I hear a heartbeat. It's faint."

"Atlas."

"I hope so." I started across the courtyard to a central building, following my ears.

It was a two-story structure built of rough stone with small glass windows. It had to be at least a few hundred years old, though my knowledge of architecture was iffy.

We were almost to the building when a small wooden door opened. A nearly skeletal man appeared. Though he was tall—well over six feet—most of his muscle had wasted away, and his eyes looked sunken in their sockets.

"Atlas?" I asked.

He stared hard at us for a moment, then nodded. "Come in."

He turned and retreated into the building, moving slowly.

I shared a glance with Maximus, catching the worry in his eyes.

We followed Atlas into the building. My eyes took a second to adjust to the darkness, and I realized we were standing in a small foyer. Atlas was still retreating down the hall, and it only took a moment for us to catch up. The whole place smelled dusty, and I doubted he came here often.

"Come, we must talk immediately." The words sounded like they'd cost him half his energy.

We followed him into an old kitchen that looked like it'd been modified only slightly from its original form a few hundred years ago. Atlas went to a worn old dining room table in front of a nearly dead hearth. Maximus knelt by the hearth and stoked the fire. As the warmth billowed out, Atlas sighed.

Though he looked to be in his sixties, the illness that had wasted him made him look far older. What the hell was he doing up here alone if he was so sick?

I sat next to Atlas, and Maximus joined us.

Atlas stared at us. "Why are you here?"

"I'm Rowan, an Amazon and a DragonGod." Wow, it sounded kinda cool when I said it out loud. I explained about the Amazons and the Stryx. My heart twisted as I thought of the Amazons, wasting away. They did so much good in the world, and now they could just...die. I finished with, "And I think you're sick for the same reason. I want to help."

He nodded slowly. "You're right, it's all connected."

"Why are you all the way out here, alone, if you're so sick?" Maximus asked the question that had been burning in my mind.

Atlas shrugged. "Because of what the Stryx are doing. That hole they're blowing into the earth is their attempt to break into Tartarus and release the titans."

My stomach dropped. "*What?*"

"You heard me. They're trying to release the monsters within. I don't know why, but I felt it as soon as they blew the first crater into the ground there."

That really could end the world. The titans were monstrously powerful. If the Stryx got ahold of them, we were all screwed. Starting with that village near the entrance to Tartarus. They'd destroy that first. The memory of the boy and his dog flashed in my mind.

"How can you feel that they are trying to get into Tartarus?" Maximus asked.

"The layer of stone that covers Tartarus acts as the gate to their prison. It keeps them trapped by the weight and strength of the stone, but also by the magic imbued within the stone. Every bit of rock that is blown away weakens the gate." He shook his head, as if remembering terrible things. "I was cursed to hold up the heavens instead of joining my brethren in Tartarus. Long ago, I escaped that fate. Zeus and the other gods weren't pleased. If I wasn't holding up the heavens, they wanted me thrown in Tartarus. The same with Prometheus, who also escaped his torture. It was too late for the gods to reopen Tartarus and put us in, but they cast a spell that ensured that if the gate to Tartarus was ever opened again, I would be sucked in. As the gate to Tartarus is broken, it pulls on me, weakening me and making me sick."

"And the Amazons, too?" I asked, my heart thundering.

"We're connected, so what happens to me, could happen to

them. And I also believe that the gods placed the same spell on them, though I don't know it for sure."

Jeez, that sucked. The Greek gods really were a piece of work, and I was one of them. Sort of. Trapped in the middle between the Amazons and the gods. This new life of mine wasn't as simple as I'd expected, but then, life rarely was.

"Don't they realize you do important work, keeping the magic that's in space from interfering with the satellites?" Maximus asked. "They aren't just modern conveniences. Militaries rely on those satellites, and if they all go down at once, at least one of those militaries will interpret it as an act of war. A seer has prophesied that World War III could start if the satellites fail."

"Their vendettas are more important to them than human wars. Even human wars that would cost millions of lives." He looked at me. "And I believe they are counting on you to stop this. That is why you are the Dragon God. And this is your hero's challenge."

I nodded, swallowing hard. "How much longer can you hold the satellites up?"

"I'm weakening. It's taking everything I've got to protect the satellites from the magic in space. But they're starting to malfunction. When they go out entirely, the world's militaries will go on high alert. War will follow soon after. You have a few days, at most."

I didn't tell him about the call from Ana that had confirmed it. "So why are you up here? You should be down where you can get help with staying strong and fighting your illness."

"The only way to help me is to close the gate to Tartarus. I can't do that myself, because if I get anywhere near it, it will suck me in. I built this place ages ago and imbued it with magic that would prevent that. But the pull is strong. I lost my strength far faster than I expected. I've been sending messages to the

Amazons and Prometheus, but I don't think they are getting through."

"So you've been trapped here, wasting away," I said.

"And quickly." He frowned. "I thought this fortress was a good idea. In a way, it was. But it hasn't gone as I planned."

"Things rarely do." I studied him. "So if we close the gate to Tartarus, you and the Amazons will get better?"

"I believe so."

Oh, thank fates. "Can you feel if the Stryx have already broken all the way through to Tartarus?" I swallowed hard, chills racing down my arms. This was the million-dollar question. "Have they released any of the titans?"

He shook his head. "I cannot tell. Perhaps they have."

"Do you know what they intend to do with them?" Maximus asked.

"No." Atlas's voice turned grave. "But it cannot be good. You need to stop them before they release them. If they haven't already."

"There's a barrier around their operation," I said. "Some kind of force field that only I can penetrate."

"If they'll allow you to cross, then I believe they must need you," Atlas said.

"But why would they need *me*?"

"You're powerful, Rowan. Your magic is powerful." Atlas shrugged. "Maybe they want that. It could help them get the titans out, perhaps."

"So they want my magic." My mind started to whir, spinning as I considered that. "They've got something that drags me to them if I get close to the barrier. I can't fight it."

Atlas frowned. "It could be that the barrier itself contains the magic to compel you to enter and stay within. There is an ancient Greek spell that can do that."

I shared a glance with Maximus. "Makes sense. They couldn't compel me to come to them before."

He nodded. "You need to stay far away from that barrier."

But I couldn't. Not if I was the only one who could get through it. Somehow, I was key to this.

Atlas leaned toward me. "You were fated for this task, Rowan. You must find a way to get past the barrier and stop them. It is your duty as a DragonGod. Your magic is the key to all of this."

I nodded. "Okay. I can do this."

And I really thought I could. Because now, I had an idea.

We'd learned pretty much all we could from Atlas, so it was time to return to the Protectorate. He escorted us out to the courtyard, stopping at the exit of his building. "I'm sorry, but you can't transport directly from here. Protective measure."

I tried not to wince. "So we have to rappel down?"

"I'm afraid so." He pointed behind him. "But if you go to the other side of the compound, there's a rope for that. Once I know you've made it, I'll pull it back up."

"Do you have the strength?"

"I will, if you close the gate to Tartarus. And if you don't... Well, it won't matter who finds me."

I nodded. "We'll do it. Stay safe."

"The same to you." He inclined his head, then disappeared back into the house.

I felt terrible leaving him. "Wait! Atlas."

He turned.

"Can we send someone to you to help you manage around here?" I didn't know who, but I was sure the Protectorate would have some contacts for someone who could help.

He smiled slightly. "I will be fine. Best you hurry with the Stryx, though."

I nodded, and Maximus and I left.

"That was helpful," Maximus said as we climbed the stairs to the top of the wall at the back of the fortress. "But I think I expected more."

"So did I. But there was one thing he said, and I think it's the key to all of this. Something we didn't realize."

"What's that?"

"The Stryx want my magic, and it's the only way to get through the barrier. I'm going to give it to them. Only, they're not going to like what they get."

CHAPTER FOURTEEN

Getting down the side of the pillar of rock was easier than climbing up, thank fates. As soon as we landed on the bottom, Maximus pulled a transport charm from his pocket.

"This is the last of them," he said.

"Like, the last, the last?" Damn. They were really hard to come by. But we'd been burning through his stash like they were kindling.

"Yeah. I'll try to get some more, but it's a good thing we've got this almost figured out."

"I think we do. Now, let's get back to the Protectorate."

Maximus threw the charm to the ground, and the familiar cloud of silvery smoke exploded upward. I stepped in, letting the ether suck me toward Scotland.

When I stepped out onto the main lawn in front of the castle, I shivered. It was colder up here, the moon already risen and the castle windows gleaming with a warm light. It seemed quieter than normal, probably because most of the staff were at the Stryx's operation, trying to break in or figure out what was going on.

I pressed my finger to my comms charm to ignite the magic. "Bree? Ana? I'm back, and I have a plan."

In unison, their voices crackled out of the charm.

"We're here, too," Bree said.

"Meet us in the entry hall," Ana added.

Maximus and I hurried across the lawn and up the castle stairs, stepping into the warmth of the main entry hall. The Cats of Catastrophe, three feline residents of the castle and Ana's familiars, raced up the stairs in a line, clearly on the hunt.

Ana and Bree appeared at the stairs leading up from the kitchen, each holding a cup of juice.

"We just got back from recon," Bree said. "The rubble pile from the Stryx's explosions is nearly to the village."

I swallowed hard, remembering the boy and his dog. "Is Jude here? And Hedy?"

"They're downstairs, too, finishing up."

"We'll join you." My stomach grumbled at the idea. "It's as good a place as any."

They nodded, and we followed them down the stairs into the warmth of Hans's domain. He was bustling around the stove, his white chef's hat perched jauntily on his head. The fire roared, illuminating Jude and Hedy, who were finishing off bowls of stew.

Jude looked up, her face haggard and her eyes tired. "Rowan. I'm glad you're safe."

Hedy smiled, too, and honestly, she didn't look any better than Jude. Her lavender hair was tangled, and matching purple shadows hung under her eyes.

Maximus and I had been chasing answers, but they hadn't been relaxing here, that was for sure.

"Any luck?" Jude asked. "Your sisters say you have a plan."

I sat across from her. "I do."

"Good." Her gaze turned dark. "Because we're running out of time."

"Eat!" Hans smacked a big bowl of stew down in front of me, along with a cup of juice. "You can have a juice box for the road, once you've finished that."

I almost laughed at the sheer normalcy of his comment in the face of all that was happening. There were a lot of things I could tell everyone about our journey, but that wasn't what I wanted to focus on.

I leaned forward. "This bomb you made, Hedy. How does it work, exactly? How big is it?"

"It's about the size of a softball," she said. "But it's currently hooked up to a magical battery the size of a vacuum cleaner. Once it's removed from the battery, it has about ten seconds until it will detonate. Once it does, it will disrupt the magical signature that creates the barrier and destroy it. Hopefully."

"Ten seconds, huh?"

"Don't think you can run it in there," Jude said. "Even if you could run fast enough and far enough—or drive, in that buggy of yours—you'd be too close to the Stryx. They could capture you. Especially since their magic calls to you now."

I nodded, agreeing with her that me running the bomb in was a crap plan. "Atlas thinks that the magic that compels me to go to the Stryx is part of the barrier."

"It's a compelling argument," Maximus said. "Since they didn't have that ability before, it's likely part of the barrier. There's also an ancient Greek spell that could help them create a barrier like that."

Jude pursed her lips. Then she nodded. "I like this logic."

"So if we can get rid of the barrier, they can't call you to them," Bree said.

I nodded. "I think so. Maybe."

Jude leaned forward. "Did you learn anything else? Like why the hell they're blowing big holes into the earth?"

I nodded, knowing she wasn't going to like this bit. "They're trying to release the titans."

"Those murderous monsters?" Jude sat back, her face white. "It sounds like they're raising an army."

I nodded. "Well, I've got a plan to break down their barrier and stop them." I leaned in and shared my idea.

From the looks on everyone's faces, they liked it.

"We need to move," Jude said. "Rowan, if you'll get what you need to break down the barrier, I'll rally the troops. We attack as soon as we're ready."

We split up, and I hurried to my room. It was as cluttered as usual, and the Menacing Menagerie was lounging on my couch, each fast asleep.

"Guys! Wake up. We're going to war."

The three of them popped up, immediately awake. Excitement gleamed in Eloise's eyes, and Poppy adjusted her flower, as if she wanted to look good for the fight.

Now? Romeo asked.

"In ten minutes. I just need to grab something." I went to the big chest that sat in the corner of the living room and knelt by it, then sucked in a deep breath.

I hated looking in this chest. It contained a reminder of what I'd lost.

But that didn't matter. Losing this magic and then gaining more from the gods had taught me one thing—I wasn't my magic. I was so much more than that. I was perseverance and toughness and the ability to pick myself up when I was down.

That's what really mattered. Not some magic trapped in a dumb rock. I'd use this to my advantage. I wouldn't let the Rebel Gods get the best of me.

I opened the chest and lifted out the rock that contained my magic. It pricked against my fingertips, feeling both familiar and foreign. In a way, it felt good. It was my magic.

But then, I knew it was tainted. I could *feel* it.

The Rebel Gods' darkness was in there.

Fortunately, I didn't think that would matter. This rock contained my magic, and that was all we really needed for this plan to work.

~

It was time for war.

Wind whipped my hair back as the buggy raced up the mountainside in central Greece. It was still nighttime, but the moon was full and bright, providing more than enough light for the battle ahead.

Ana drove the buggy, while Bree stood with me on the front platform. Maximus, Cade, and Lachlan took the back platform, ready to fight. The Menacing Menagerie rode in the back seat, ready to jump out when the battle started. Members of the Protectorate were ascending the mountainside all around, headed for the crater at the top. When I broke down the barrier, they'd flood in and take out the Stryx's demon army.

That was the plan, at least.

"We're getting close!" Bree shouted. "You ready?"

I shifted the magic-filled rock in my hand. It was a little smaller than a basketball, and we'd attached a massive slingshot to the front platform of the buggy. It was suspended between two rods that stuck up from the railings. Then, we'd taped the small bomb to the side of the rock. The bomb was still plugged into the battery, which was basically just a huge glowing rock filled with sparkling magic that powered the explosive force Hedy had packed into the bomb. We'd strapped the battery into the passenger seat, but when we yanked the cord and shot the thing past the barrier...

Boom.

The buggy bounced over a massive rock, and I grabbed the railing, holding on tightly as Ana got us on the right course. We crested the ridge, and I caught sight of Ali and Haris about a hundred yards away, crouched on the edge of the ridge, waiting. Caro was with them, her bright platinum hair covered by a dark hat. If I squinted, I could see dozens more, including members of the Order who'd joined up for the final battle.

"I sure hope this works," I muttered to Bree.

"It's a good plan. It will work."

"Only a hundred yards away now," Ana shouted.

Gravel kicked up from behind the wheels as the buggy plowed down the mountainside toward the barrier. I could feel it prickle against my skin. Worse, I felt the call of the Stryx. It tugged at me, wanting to yank me toward them.

My hand went to the chain wrapped around my waist. It was connected to the front platform of the buggy. I had about thirty yards of slack if I needed it, but the chain was just a little safety precaution in case the call of the Stryx became too strong and I ran toward them like a crazy person.

I shook my head, trying to drive off the feel of being bound to them.

"Twenty yards!" Ana shouted.

I could see the barrier now, just slightly. It was barely darker than the air around it, a hazy gray. When we were only five yards away, Ana pulled the wheel hard to the right, and the buggy turned, driving alongside the barrier.

"Ready?" Bree asked.

"So ready." I wanted to get rid of my tainted magic. Hurl it at the Stryx and use what they wanted against them.

I fitted the rock into the slingshot pouch, then pulled back. I leaned hard away from the railing, getting as much tension as I could on the slingshot. We needed this thing to fly *far*.

My muscles trembled as I pulled. "Now."

Bree yanked the battery cord free. "Ten seconds!"

I released the slingshot, and the rock shot forward. I held my breath, praying my plan would work. When the rock sailed through the barrier, I couldn't help but grin.

It had worked.

The Stryx had wanted my magic. Well, they'd get it. And a whole lot more.

I counted down the seconds, praying the explosion went off. Silence reigned as everyone stared forward. Waiting, waiting.

I bit my lip, staring hard into the darkness.

Finally, it came. The flash of light nearly blinded me, followed shortly after by a boom that made my ears ring. I blinked through the brightness, spotting dozens of blue streaks of light coming from the middle of the crater.

They shot toward the domed barrier, lighting it up. They threaded through the dome, making it look like a cage.

"It's weakening," Bree said.

"But it hasn't fallen yet." I frowned. "Maybe we could run through it, but..."

The bolts of blue light crackled within the dome. The energy in the bomb was breaking down the barrier, but it wasn't quite strong enough. It needed more juice.

An idea came. It was crazy, but...

"Ana, stop the buggy!" I shouted.

"Are you crazy?"

"Yes! But I have an idea."

She pressed on the brakes, and I grabbed the railing of the front platform for support. As soon as the buggy stopped, I jumped off the platform.

"What are you doing?" Maximus shouted.

"Don't worry." I shook the chain that was tied around my waist. "I can't get far."

Then I called upon the lightning within me. It streaked through my veins, making me light up with energy that tore through my muscles. Pain followed, but I ignored it, letting the lightning crackle through me until I was a human lightning bolt. When I was sure that I was as lit up as I could be, I sprinted for the barrier.

I plowed through it, feeling it crackle and break as I plowed through. The chain pulled me up short, and I stopped, panting.

I let the lightning fade from my body, immediately feeling the pull of the Stryx. They called me to them, making my muscles want to move in their direction.

I fought it, breathing deeply as I looked up.

The barrier was breaking away.

My lightning blast had given the spell the last bit of energy it needed, and the dome was retreating. Blue light from the bomb still crackled within it, and it was beautiful.

Slowly, the pull of the Stryx faded.

Oh, thank fates.

"Rowan!" Bree shouted. "Let's go!"

I felt a tug on my chain, and turned. Everyone watched expectantly from the buggy. All around, members of the Protectorate and the Order of the Magica flowed down the hill into the crater.

With the barrier gone, the fight could begin.

I sprinted back to the buggy and scrambled up onto the front platform.

"Their pull has disappeared," I said, yanking at the chain around my waist.

Bree helped me get it off, and Ana hit the gas, speeding forward. Though the barrier was gone, the Stryx hadn't stopped their digging. Explosions still tore through the night, the sound deafening. Debris flew into the air from their operations, dark smoke and tiny bits of volcanic rock raining down. I squinted through it, trying to spot our enemy.

When I did, I gasped.

There were so many.

Demons of all varieties. Big and small, skinny and muscular. Some with huge weapons and others with magic glowing around their claws, ready to be hurled at us.

"Slow down!" I shouted at Ana. We were about to reach the spot where the crater bottomed out and we'd lose our height advantage for reconnaissance. "We need to find the Stryx."

Ana slowed the buggy, and we searched through the shifting smoke. It moved as giant clouds, concealing and revealing the demon army.

To our right and left, fighters from our side sprinted toward the demons. Ali and Haris led the charge, the two djinns running full out. They sprinted straight at the two biggest demons. Before the monsters could strike, the djinns ran straight into them, possessing them. Immediately, the giants turned on the demons around them, swinging their massive clubs at their fellow soldiers. The clubs sent the demons flying like they were dominos.

Caro followed, holding out her hands and shooting water straight into the chest of a demon who ran for her. The water was so fast that it struck the demon like a blade, plowing through him and coming out of his back, tinged pink with blood.

I searched for the Stryx, finally spotting them through the haze. I pointed. "There!"

"Got it!" Ana hit the gas, and we surged forward.

Hundreds of demons stood between us and the Stryx.

Bree stepped forward, hands raised. Lightning struck from

the sky, clearing a path right in front of the buggy. Demons ran, and the buggy plowed through.

They attacked from the sides, firing bolts of magic toward us. A blast of fire headed toward me, and I dived low, skidding on the front platform as it zipped over my head. The heat singed my hair.

Two more demons leapt toward the front platform, grabbing the railing and trying to climb on. As I jumped to my feet, I conjured a sword and swiped at their hands, cutting them free. They howled as they fell.

Time for the show to start! Romeo leapt off of the buggy, clinging to the head of a demon.

The beast roared as Romeo went for his eyes.

Eloise and Poppy followed, both pulling a similar trick on two more demons and going for their eyes.

More demons surged for the back platform, so many that they were climbing over each other to board the vehicle.

"It's too small to fight from here!" Lachlan shouted. Magic swirled around him, and he shifted into his black lion form. He jumped off the vehicle, straight into the crowd of demons. He was so powerful that blood began to fly immediately.

Cade followed, shifting into his huge wolf form. Together, they made a formidable army. Maximus stayed on the back, his sword drawn and always moving. He was so fast and so graceful, cutting down the demons before they could board.

Ana kept her foot on the gas, plowing past the demons who attacked.

As we neared and the dust cleared further, I saw that they weren't alone. Three massive figures surrounded them. They were three times the height of a normal person, and looked haggard and angry.

"Holy fates, they've got some of the titans." Ice chilled my skin as I surveyed the scene.

The titans surrounded the Stryx like a barrier. Within their protective circle, the Stryx operated something that looked like a giant ray gun. It was sitting on legs that had been bolted into the ground and fired blasts of magic into the earth. Every time it fired, magic exploded out of it, shooting straight into Tartarus.

As I watched, horrified, another titan climbed out of the earth. Holy fates.

"We're too late," Bree said. "They've got them out already."

CHAPTER FIFTEEN

"They've only got four," I said. "There are still a lot more."

Bree called upon her lightning, directing it at the titan nearest us. The bolt struck him right in the head, but he just grinned. He looked like he was hewn from rock itself, so the effect was eerie.

"Crap." She scowled.

Beside us, a continent of mages from the Protectorate advanced on a troop of demons that stood between them and the titans. The mages threw blasts of flame and ice. Their barrage was so forceful that the demons were forced backward. They piled up in front of the titan that Bree had attacked with lightning.

He grinned again, a horrible facsimile of a smile, then raised his foot and stomped on the demons. He crushed five of them with one step, then raised his foot again and crushed some more. Within ten seconds, he'd killed forty.

"Holy fates." My skin paled. He was enormous and fast and bloodthirsty.

And we were screwed.

"How are we going to get past them?" Ana shouted.

We couldn't. There was absolutely no way we could fight our way past that titan and survive. Especially not since there were now four of them. At least one of us would die.

But I could get in.

I turned to my friends. "I have an idea."

Ana frowned. "I don't like the look on your face."

"They need me. They'll let me in. I'll disable the drill if you'll distract the titans. Bree and Ana, could you provide support from the air?"

"No." Maximus's voice was hard. "It's too dangerous."

"It's the only way to get past them."

"It's not."

"It's the only safe way. You can still try to fight your way past once I'm in. But I need to get in there *now*. More titans will come out. We can't let that happen." I leapt out of the buggy, ignoring their shouts.

As fast as I could, I raced toward the Stryx. I knew I had to do this. Maybe it was premonition or something, but I *knew*.

All around, the battle raged. Mages against demons, our side against theirs. With the titans overseeing it all, protecting the Stryx and stomping on anyone who got too close, it was a lopsided battle.

I was going to change that, however.

I drew my shield and electric sword from the ether, blocking a fireball sent by a flame red demon. The force of it reverberated through the shield, and I grunted, nearly going down to one knee. A second later, a lightning bolt struck the demon who'd attacked me.

Bree.

I sprinted faster, cutting through the horde of demons. Massive boulders that had been blasted out of the ground provided cover, but not much of it. I darted around them. Ahead of me, dirt heaved upward, rolling over the demons who stood in my way. A path was formed, right to the Stryx. Ana was moving the earth.

My sisters might've thought I was crazy, but they had my back.

As I neared, a titan turned its red gaze on me. I swallowed hard, fear icing my skin.

Holy fates, this was scary.

"Hey, you bastard!" I shouted, trying to catch the attention of the Stryx without being too obvious about it. "Come at me! I'm an Amazon! A freaking DragonGod!"

Yeah, it was a lot of bragging, but it made it clear who I was. And I'd bet that bragging wasn't out of the norm for the Stryx, so they probably wouldn't think it was too weird.

The titan growled, and it sounded like boulders rubbing together. He raised a foot right over me, and I started to dart out of the way.

"Wait!" The shriek carried across the battlefield, so powerful and loud that I winced. "We need her! Bring her to us!"

Jackpot.

I ran a bit to make it look real, but when the titan picked me up, I grinned. As the titan's hand squeezed me, terror drove the smile, but this was all part of the plan. I just had to remember that.

Please work, plan.

The titan's grip was strong, and I could barely breathe as he swung me toward the Stryx and their giant magical drill. Even up close, it looked like a massive ray gun propped on sturdy metal legs, pointing right into the ground. From up here, I could see straight into the scar in the earth where they'd drilled toward Tartarus. It glowed with red and black magic, stinking of sulfur and rage.

The titan tossed me on the rocks near the magical drill, and I rolled, pain singing through my shoulder and hip.

I leapt upward, but was too slow. The Stryx grabbed me by both arms and thrust me toward the drill. Chains whipped out from the drill and twisted around me, tying me to the body of the thing.

"Let go!" I thrashed, trying to break free, but the Stryx just laughed in unison.

Their dark hair floated around their heads and their purple eyes gleamed with satisfaction. They were dressed for battle in black fatigues, clearly having updated their wardrobe.

At my back, the drill continued to shoot blasts of magic into the ground, breaking away the earth that formed the gate to Tartarus.

"You're just what we needed." The Stryx on the right grinned evilly as she reached up toward the body of the drill and pulled something down. I couldn't see it, but when she jammed it into my arm, I sure felt it.

"Ouch!" I tried to lash out at her, but my hands were bound down by my stomach.

"Stupid," the Stryx muttered.

She backed up, and her sister followed. I looked down at my arm, my heart thundering. A glowing crystal blade had been plunged into my bicep, and it hurt like hell.

"What the hell is this thing?" I demanded.

The Stryx ignored me.

All around, the battle raged. On one side, I spotted some of my sisters' friends—women I liked, though I didn't know them well. The FireSouls from Magic's Bend. Cass, Del, and Nix. They fought a titan, keeping him occupied with illusions of another giant who was out to get him. I could see Cass casting the illusions from behind the cover provided by a pile of rocks. Nix conjured huge boulders for the titan to trip over, while Del stayed demons all around him.

To my right, Cade and Lachlan fought one of the titans in

their wolf and lion forms, respectively. They leapt for the beast's throat, distracting it with their agility and ferocity.

Caro, Ali, Haris, and Jude distracted another titan. The women attacked with water and an electric whip, while Ali and Haris tried to possess the great monster. If they could manage, that would be a major coup for our side. I didn't have time to watch and see.

The last titan battle caught my eye.

Maximus fought one single-handedly. He charged at the one who'd stomped on all the demons, leaping up into the air to land a solid kick to the giant's chest.

The titan toppled backward, overpowered by Maximus's strength. Maximus then began to push the demon toward the pit that led to Tartarus. I almost cheered him on, but then a stab of pain sliced through my arm from the blade.

It sucked at me, pulling at my magic. Feeding it into the magical drill.

Oh, hell no.

That was why they needed me. My magic was supposed to power their gun, probably to break away the last bit of barrier to Tartarus.

I struggled to tear free, unwilling to let it happen. The Stryx watched with delight as their dumb machine broke into the earth. My heart thundered as my mind raced for an escape plan.

Out of the corner of my eye, I spotted the buggy, which had been abandoned in the middle of the battlefield.

Help was coming.

I looked up, searching for my sisters.

They hovered high above, Bree with her silver Valkyrie wings and Ana in her giant crow form.

As if on cue, they dive-bombed the Stryx.

Ana led with her beak, going for the head of one of the Stryx, while Bree swiped her sword at the other.

I left them to it, struggling to reach for my potion belt. If I could just get that little vial...

I strained every muscle, reaching for it. The sound of battle raged as my fingertips closed around the vial. I pulled it free, struggling to uncork it. The stopper popped out, and I nearly wept with gratitude.

As carefully as I could, I poured a droplet of the liquid on the chain that wrapped around my waist and wrist. It burned through it immediately, a droplet falling on my leg.

I hissed at the pain, then forced it from my mind. I had a little more movement with my arm now, and I managed to pour a couple more droplets that freed me entirely.

I broke away from the chains just as the Stryx fired massive blasts of flame at my sisters. I yanked the stupid blade from my arm that was sucking out my magic and screamed, "Go!"

Bree and Ana darted for the sky, avoiding the fireballs by inches.

I sprinted for the Stryx, my arms outstretched. They looked the worse for wear from my sisters' surprise attacks. A gash decorated the cheek of one, and another wore an ugly wound on her shoulder.

They stood so close together that I managed to grab them both at the same time, bowling us over in a pile.

I didn't even hesitate as I called on the power of Hades. I had to weaken them enough that they couldn't attack me with their magic. And they wouldn't see this power coming.

Immediately, my death magic sucked on their life force, draining it out of them. As it flowed into me, I gagged.

So dirty.

I nearly let go, but the fear in their eyes kept me going.

This was working.

I could kill them this way.

But their life force...

It was disgusting. I nearly choked as I kept it up, trying to drain them dry.

Beneath me, they bucked, struggling to break free. They shrieked for the titans, but none came. All around me, I could hear the battle raging as my friends distracted their bodyguards.

I clung to them, desperate to finish the job.

Terror gave them strength, and they finally managed to throw me off. I landed hard on my side, the wound in my shoulder burning.

The Stryx leapt up and scrambled away, terror widening their eyes. The one on the left threw a huge blast of flame at me, but I managed to roll away just in time.

The one on the right dug into her pocket and withdrew acid green charms. She hurled one of them to the right, and I caught sight of it fly toward a titan who was still battling Cade and Lachlan.

The charm slammed against the titan's back, and he disappeared.

Shit! They were running for it.

"Intercept the green transport charms!" I screamed as I scrambled to my feet, but I knew it was too late. My voice couldn't compete with the roar of battle, and the Stryx were fast.

They hit two more titans, who disappeared immediately, but they missed the one that Maximus shoved back into the pit into Tartarus.

I sprinted for the Stryx, but they joined hands, glaring at me. The Stryx on the left slammed the green charm into her chest. They disappeared a half second later.

I wanted to shriek my frustration and fall to the ground, but I couldn't.

The magical drill was still firing.

I turned and ran for it, but Bree and Ana had gotten there first. They flew into it, pushing it over and breaking it in half.

All around, my friends and allies finished off the demons who remained. There were no more titans. No more Stryx.

Not here, at least.

My sisters landed in front of me, Ana shifting back into human form as she set foot on the ground.

"We need to get to work," she said. "Let's close up this gate."

I nodded, swallowing my disappointment at losing the Stryx. We had work to do before the threat was gone.

"I'll clear the field." Bree launched herself into the air, flying from fighter to fighter, commanding them to clear out.

The earth mages stayed, along with anyone else who could help.

I sprinted to the buggy, then leapt into the driver's seat and cranked the engine. Before they completely destroyed the crater, I wanted to get the magical drill out of here. It was broken, but no way I wanted it repurposed by the titans in Tartarus. And we might learn something from it, though it was unlikely.

I stopped the buggy next to the drill and climbed onto the front platform, grabbing the chain that had so recently been tied around my waist. My arm ached as I worked, but not as badly as my disappointment.

"I've got this." Maximus appeared at my side, taking the chain from my hands. He met my gaze, worry in his eyes. "Are you okay?"

"I'm good."

"Promise?"

"Promise." There was more I wanted to say to him, but now wasn't the time. I nodded to the chain. "Thanks for that."

I climbed back into the driver's seat as he wrapped the chain around the broken drill.

Once he'd finished, he walked over to the driver's side. "I'm going to stay and help with this. I'll see you in a bit."

"See you." I pressed on the gas and drove away from the pit, dragging the magical drill behind me. On my way up to the edge of the crater, I stopped to pick up the wounded.

Caro the water mage had a nasty bump on her head, her platinum hair stained red. Jude looked like she might have a broken arm, but her blue eyes gleamed with victory. Ali and Haris were fine, so they waved me on.

The Menacing Menagerie were busy raiding the demon corpses before they disappeared and returned to their hells, so they just ignored me. I picked up a few people I didn't recognize, but at least all of them looked like they would live.

At the top of the crater, I turned back to look.

Maximus was rolling the enormous boulders back into the pit, while the earth mages were commanding huge piles of rubble to pour back into Tartarus. Ana stood amongst them, moving more earth than anyone.

"We did well," Jude said.

I turned to look at her. "I let the Stryx get away."

"You didn't let them. They ran scared. They were terrified of you."

She was right. They had been. "They're still gone. And they've got three titans."

"Better than twelve. And if we closed the gate to Tartarus in time and Atlas heals, we'll have saved the satellites and avoided WWIII. I consider that a win."

I nodded. "I suppose you're right. Live to fight another day."

And the Amazons would be okay. That was a *huge* win. We'd use these victories to defeat the Stryx. We could do it. They were afraid of me. I was going to make sure they stayed that way.

CHAPTER SIXTEEN

An hour later, after dropping off the wounded and the magical drill, I returned to the mountain in Greece. The sun was rising, and it was light enough that I could see the village at the bottom of the mountain.

The rubble pile that had nearly crushed it was gone. All of that was piled back in the pit that led to Tartarus. Wearily, I climbed the hill toward the top. I could still hear the scraping of earth as they finished filling in the hole, and I prayed that the Obsidia wouldn't make an appearance. I didn't have the energy to face the little bastards.

When I reached the top, a smile stretched across my face for the first time in a while. The pit was gone. So was the crater. Maximus, Ana, and Bree climbed up the shallow slope toward me, along with a half dozen other mages who'd helped put the earth back into place now that the barrier no longer prevented us.

Gratitude swelled in my chest as I looked at my sisters. They all looked whole and healthy, though pretty dinged up. But in our world, anything short of on-your-back-dying was pretty good.

Maximus walked straight up to me and didn't even hesitate. He just wrapped his arm around me and pulled me toward him. I melted into his warmth, so damned happy that he was safe. There hadn't been time before. Closing the gate to Tartarus was too important. But now that I had a second, I focused on him.

I leaned back and pressed a quick kiss to his lips. "Good job with that titan."

"That little guy? Nothing." He grinned.

I smiled back, then turned to my sisters. Bree leaned against Cade, while Ana leaned against Lachlan.

"Do you think this thing is closed for good?" I asked.

"All of the earth is back on top of it," Bree said.

"The Order will send mages to enchant it," Maximus said. "It needs to be reinforced with magic."

I nodded, remembering what Atlas had said about the magic that kept the titans in place. It wasn't just the earth. But hopefully, with the ground covered back up, the Amazons and Atlas would be fine.

Ana dug into her pocket, then pulled out a rock. She held it out to me. "Here. You can go check on the Amazons. I know you were worried about them."

I nodded gratefully and took the transport charm. "I am."

I hugged her and Bree, then pulled back. "Want to meet at my place later tonight for a drink?"

They grinned. "I think we deserve a little celebrating."

"I hope so." I wouldn't feel like it until I knew the Amazons and Atlas were okay.

We said goodbye, then I turned to Maximus. "I think I need to do this alone."

He nodded, a slight smile on his face. He leaned in to speak into my ear. "Perhaps we could have that date when you get back? In a few days, once you've recovered."

Warmth flowed through me. "Yes." I didn't even hesitate. "I'd like that."

He stepped back and pressed a kiss to my cheek, then turned to leave.

I waved goodbye to my sisters, then threw the transport charm to the ground. It exploded upward in a plume of silver dust. I stepped into it, letting the ether suck me in and spin me through space, then depositing me in a busy street in Istanbul. The sun was higher here, and the day warmer.

I hurried down the sidewalk, toward the Amazons' building. As soon as I entered the tall glass building, my gaze went to the two guards who sat at the table, once again playing chess.

They stood. No golden crystals hung around their necks.

"Are you better?" I demanded. "Has the wasting disease gone away?"

They both grinned widely. "As of a half hour ago."

I sagged in relief, my muscles nearly turning to water. "Oh, thank fates. How is everyone else? The Queens? Atlas?"

"The Queens want to see you."

I nodded, following them to the elevator. Tension crawled over my skin as the elevator rose. I ignored the view of the city and focused on the Amazons. "How is everyone?"

The dark-haired Amazon turned to me, a wide smile stretching across her face. "Better. It was like the strength all flowed back into us at once."

The door dinged open, and I hurried out.

Queen Penthesilea and Queen Hippolyta surged to their feet.

"You were successful," Queen Hippolyta said.

I strode toward them, taking in their vibrant expressions. There were no charms around their necks. Thank fates. I'd been so worried about them.

They were an ancient race dedicated to protecting the world, and they'd almost been wiped out. Not to mention, they were the last of my kind.

I couldn't help myself.

I threw out my arms and hugged them both.

They stood stiffly for only half a second, as if confused, then they wrapped their arms around me and hugged me back. Warmth flowed through me.

I had my family—my sisters were my family, no question about it. But I could always use more. If my time in captivity had taught me anything, it was that I could always use more good in my life. More family and friends.

I pulled back. "You're really all right?"

Queen Penthesilea nodded. "So is Atlas. He sent a message fifteen minutes ago. He's well, and the satellites should be too."

"And Prometheus?"

"We haven't heard from him," Queen Hippolyta said. "But then, we wouldn't normally. We assume he is okay."

"Probably pulling a con on someone else," I said.

They gave me quizzical looks, but I ignored them. No need to tell them the story of how Prometheus might have manipulated me into drinking a ridiculous amount of Raki all while intending to help me.

Queen Hippolyta stepped back. "Would you like to meet some of the other Amazons? Now that we're not under such a tight and dire time schedule?"

"I'd love that." And I really would. I was going to need to learn a lot if I wanted to defeat the Stryx.

THANK YOU FOR READING!

I hope you enjoyed reading this book as much as I enjoyed writing it. Reviews are *so* helpful to authors. I really appreciate all reviews, both positive and negative. If you want to leave one, you can do so on Amazon or GoodReads.

Join my mailing list at www.linseyhall.com/subscribe to stay updated and to get a free ebook copy of *Death Valley Magic,* the story of the Dragon God's early adventures. Turn the page for an excerpt.

EXCERPT OF DEATH VALLEY MAGIC

Death Valley Junction
  Eight years before the events in Undercover Magic

Getting fired sucked. Especially when it was from a place as crappy as the Death's Door Saloon.

"Don't let the door hit you on the way out," my ex-boss said.

"Screw you, Don." I flipped him the bird and strode out into the sunlight that never gave Death Valley a break.

The door slammed behind me as I shoved on my sunglasses and stomped down the boardwalk with my hands stuffed in my pockets.

What was I going to tell my sisters? We *needed* this job.

There were roughly zero freaking jobs available in this postage stamp town, and I'd just given one up because I wouldn't let the old timers pinch me on the butt when I brought them their beer.

Good going, Ana.

I kicked the dust on the ground and quickened my pace toward home, wondering if Bree and Rowan had heard from Uncle Joe yet. He wasn't blood family—we had none of that left besides each other—but he was the closest thing to it and he'd been missing for three days.

Three days was a lifetime when you were crossing Death Valley. Uncle Joe made the perilous trip about once a month, delivering outlaws to Hider's Haven. It was a dangerous trip on the best of days. But he should have been back by now.

Worry tugged at me as I made the short walk home. Death Valley Junction was a nothing town in the middle of Death Valley, the only all-supernatural city for hundreds of miles. It looked like it was right out of the old west, with low-slung wooden buildings, swinging saloon doors, and boardwalks stretching along the dirt roads.

Our house was at the end of town, a ramshackle thing that had last been repaired in the 1950s. As usual, Bree and Rowan were outside, working on the buggy. The buggy was a monster truck, the type of vehicle used to cross the valley, and it was our pride and joy.

Bree's sturdy boots stuck out from underneath the front of the truck, and Rowan was at the side, painting Ravener poison onto the spikes that protruded from the doors.

"Hey, guys."

Rowan turned. Confusion flashed in her green eyes, and she shoved her black hair back from her cheek. "Oh hell. What happened?"

"Fired." I looked down. "Sorry."

Bree rolled out from under the car. Her dark hair glinted in the sun as she stood, and grease dotted her skin where it was revealed by the strappy brown leather top she wore. We all wore the same style, since it was suited to the climate.

She squinted up at me. "I told you that you should have left that job a long time ago."

"I know. But we needed the money to get the buggy up and running."

She shook her head. "Always the practical one."

"I'll take that as a compliment. Any word from Uncle Joe?"

"Nope." Bree flicked the little crystal she wore around her neck. "He still hasn't activated his panic charm, but he should have been home days ago."

Worry clutched in my stomach. "What if he's wounded and can't activate the charm?"

Months ago, we'd forced him to start wearing the charm. He'd refused initially, saying it didn't matter if we knew he was in trouble. It was too dangerous for us to cross the valley to get him.

But that meant just leaving him. And that was crap, obviously.

We might be young, but we were tough. And we had the buggy. True, we'd never made a trip across, and the truck was only now in working order. But we were gearing up for it. We wanted to join Uncle Joe in the business of transporting outlaws across the valley to Hider's Haven.

He was the only one in the whole town brave enough to make the trip, but he was getting old and we wanted to take over for him. The pay was good. Even better, I wouldn't have to let anyone pinch me on the butt.

There weren't a lot of jobs for girls on the run. We could only be paid under the table, which made it hard.

"Even if he was wounded, Uncle Joe would find a way to activate the charm," Bree said.

As if he'd heard her, the charm around Bree's neck lit up, golden and bright.

She looked down, eyes widening. "Holy fates."

Panic sliced through me. My gaze met hers, then darted to Rowan's. Worry glinted in both their eyes.

"We have to go," Rowan said.

I nodded, my mind racing. This was *real*. We'd only ever

talked about crossing the valley. Planned and planned and planned.

But this was *go time.*

"Is the buggy ready?" I asked.

"As ready as it'll ever be," Rowan said.

My gaze traced over it. The truck was a hulking beast, with huge, sturdy tires and platforms built over the front hood and the back. We'd only ever heard stories of the monsters out in Death Valley, but we needed a place from which to fight them and the platforms should do the job. The huge spikes on the sides would help, but we'd be responsible for fending off most of the monsters.

All of the cars in Death Valley Junction looked like something out of *Mad Max*, but ours was one of the few that had been built to cross the valley.

At least, we hoped it could cross.

We had some magic to help us out, at least. I could create shields, Bree could shoot sonic booms, and Rowan could move things with her mind.

Rowan's gaze drifted to the sun that was high in the sky. "Not the best time to go, but I don't see how we have a choice."

I nodded. No one wanted to cross the valley in the day. According to Uncle Joe, it was the most dangerous of all. But things must be really bad if he'd pressed the button now.

He was probably hoping we were smart enough to wait to cross.

We weren't.

"Let's get dressed and go." I hurried up the creaky front steps and into the ramshackle house.

It didn't take long to dig through my meager possessions and find the leather pants and strappy top that would be my fight wear for out in the valley. It was too hot for anything more, though night would bring the cold.

Daggers were my preferred weapon—mostly since they were cheaper than swords and I had good aim with anything small and pointy. I shoved as many as I could into the little pockets built into the outside of my boots and pants. A small duffel full of daggers completed my arsenal.

I grabbed a leather jacket and the sand goggles that I'd gotten second hand, then ran out of the room. I nearly collided with Bree, whose blue eyes were bright with worry.

"We can do this," I said.

She nodded. "You're right. It's been our plan all along."

I swallowed hard, mind racing with all the things that could go wrong. The valley was full of monsters and dangerous challenges—and according to Uncle Joe, they changed every day. We had no idea what would be coming at us, but we couldn't turn back.

Not with Uncle Joe on the other side.

We swung by the kitchen to grab jugs of water and some food, then hurried out of the house. Rowan was already in the driver's seat, ready to go. Her sand goggles were pushed up on her head, and her leather top looked like armor.

"Get a move on!" she shouted.

I raced to the truck and scrambled up onto the back platform. Though I could open the side door, I was still wary of the Ravener poison Rowan had painted onto the spikes. It would paralyze me for twenty-four hours, and that was the last thing we needed.

Bree scrambled up to join me, and we tossed the supplies onto the floorboard of the back seat, then joined Rowan in the front, sitting on the long bench.

She cranked the engine, which grumbled and roared, then pulled away from the house.

"Holy crap, it's happening." Excitement and fear shivered across my skin.

Worry was a familiar foe. I'd been worried my whole life. Worried about hiding from the unknown people who hunted us. Worried about paying the bills. Worried about my sisters. But it'd never done me any good. So I shoved aside my fear for Uncle Joe and focused on what was ahead.

The wind tore through my hair as Rowan drove away from Death Valley Junction, cutting across the desert floor as the sun blazed down. I shielded my eyes, scouting the mountains ahead. The range rose tall, cast in shadows of gray and beige.

Bree pointed to a path that had been worn through the scrubby ground. "Try here!"

Rowan turned right, and the buggy cut toward the mountains. There was a parallel valley—the *real* Death Valley— that only supernaturals could access. That was what we had to cross.

Rowan drove straight for one of the shallower inclines, slowing the buggy as it climbed up the mountain. The big tires dug into the ground, and I prayed they'd hold up. We'd built most of the buggy from secondhand stuff, and there was no telling what was going to give out first.

The three of us leaned forward as we neared the top, and I swore I could hear our heartbeats pounding in unison. When we crested the ridge and spotted the valley spread out below us, my breath caught.

It was beautiful. And terrifying. The long valley had to be at least a hundred miles long and several miles wide. Different colors swirled across the ground, looking like they simmered with heat.

Danger cloaked the place, dark magic that made my skin crawl.

"Welcome to hell," Bree muttered.

"I kinda like it," I said. "It's terrifying but..."

"Awesome," Rowan said.

"You are both nuts," Bree said. "Now drive us down there. I'm ready to fight some monsters."

Rowan saluted and pulled the buggy over the mountain ridge, then navigated her way down the mountainside.

"I wonder what will hit us first?" My heart raced at the thought.

"Could be anything," Bree said. "Bad Water has monsters, kaleidoscope dunes has all kinds of crazy shit, and the arches could be trouble."

We were at least a hundred miles from Hider's Haven, though Uncle Joe said the distances could change sometimes. Anything could come at us in that amount of time.

Rowan pulled the buggy onto the flat ground.

"I'll take the back." I undid my seatbelt and scrambled up onto the back platform.

Bree climbed onto the front platform, carrying her sword.

"Hang on tight!" Rowan cried.

I gripped the safety railing that we'd installed on the back platform and crouched to keep my balance. She hit the gas, and the buggy jumped forward.

Rowan laughed like a loon and drove us straight into hell.

Up ahead, the ground shimmered in the sun, glowing silver.

"What do you think that is?" Rowan called.

"I don't know," I shouted. "Go around!"

She turned left, trying to cut around the reflective ground, but the silver just extended into our path, growing wider and wider. Death Valley moving to accommodate us.

Moving to trap us.

Then the silver raced toward us, stretching across the ground.

There was no way around.

"You're going to have to drive over it!" I shouted.

She hit the gas harder, and the buggy sped up. The reflective surface glinted in the sun, and as the tires passed over it, water kicked up from the wheels.

"It's the Bad Water!" I cried.

The old salt lake was sometimes dried up, sometimes not. But it wasn't supposed to be deep. Six inches, max. Right?

Please be right, Uncle Joe.

Rowan sped over the water, the buggy's tires sending up silver spray that sparkled in the sunlight. It smelled like rotten eggs, and I gagged, then breathed shallowly through my mouth.

Magic always had a signature—taste, smell, sound. Something that lit up one of the five senses. Maybe more.

And a rotten egg stink was bad news. That meant dark magic.

Tension fizzed across my skin as we drove through the Bad Water. On either side of the car, water sprayed up from the wheels in a dazzling display that belied the danger of the situation. By the time the explosion came, I was strung so tight that I almost leapt off the platform.

The monster was as wide as the buggy, but so long that I couldn't see where it began or ended. It was a massive sea creature with fangs as long as my arm and brilliant blue eyes. Silver scales were the same color as the water, which was still only six inches deep, thank fates.

Magic propelled the monster, who circled our vehicle, his body glinting in the sun. He had to be a hundred feet long, with black wings and claws. He climbed on the ground and leapt into the air, slithering around as he examined us.

"It's the Unhcegila!" Bree cried from the front.

Shit.

Uncle Joe had told us about the Unhcegila—a terrifying water monster from Dakota and Lakota Sioux legends.

Except it was real, as all good legends were. And it occasionally appeared when the Bad Water wasn't dried up. It only needed a few inches to appear.

Looked like it was our lucky day.

~~~

Join my mailing list at www.linseyhall.com/subscribe to continue the adventure and get a free copy of *Death Valley Magic*. No spam and you can leave anytime!

AUTHOR'S NOTE

Thank you for reading *Clash of Magic!* If you've made it this far, you've probably read some of my previous books and know that I like to include historical places and mythological elements in my stories. Sometimes the history of these things is so interesting that I want to share more, and I like to do it in the Author's Note instead of the story itself.

Clash of Magic was chock full of mythological elements. That's one thing that's easy about having a Greek Dragon God— we have so much information available about the Greeks and their religion. Many of the mythological elements were as I presented them in the story. For example, Atlas and Prometheus were the two titans who did not end up in Tartarus, while the Hesperides were in fact daughters of Atlas. Ladon the dragon was said to guard the golden apples in their garden, though some sources state that they were actually oranges. In this story, I wrote them as oranges.

The Amazons were said to live by the shore of the Black Sea, though I did invent the bit about them almost being thrown into Tartarus. Though they were frequent the enemies of the Greek heroes. I decided to give them a more modern spin and put them in the nearest large city to their ancestral homeland. The drink Raki that Prometheus and Rowan shared is the traditional Turkish liquor that you would find in many bars. I have not had it myself, but my Turkish friend says it is quite the intense beverage.

The location of Atlas's hideout is based upon the crazy rock formations at Meteora, in Greece. In present day, there are monasteries built on top of the rocks, but for the purposes of the story, Atlas was out there all on his lonesome.

The Oracle at Delphi is one of the most famous oracles in history. She was generally an older peasant woman from the nearby village, and she gave her prophecies from within a small round building at the temple site of Delphi. Some people believed that she spoke the words of Apollo himself.

I think that's it for the history and mythology in *Clash of Magic*—at least the big things. I hope you enjoyed the book and will come back for more of Rowan, Maximus, Ana and Bree!

To Mary Ann and Bart, with love.

ACKNOWLEDGMENTS

Thank you, Ben, for everything. There would be no books without you.

Thank you to Jena O'Connor and Lindsey Loucks for your excellent editing. Thank you to Richard Goodrum for your eagle eye with errors. The book is immensely better because of you!

Thank you to Orina Kafe for the beautiful cover art. Thank you to Collette Markwardt for allowing me to borrow the Pugs of Destruction, who are real dogs named Chaos, Havoc, and Ruckus. They were all adopted from rescue agencies.

ABOUT LINSEY

Before becoming a writer, Linsey Hall was a nautical archaeologist who studied shipwrecks from Hawaii and the Yukon to the UK and the Mediterranean. She credits fantasy and historical romances with her love of history and her career as an archaeologist. After a decade of tromping around the globe in search of old bits of stuff that people left lying about, she settled down and started penning her own romance novels. Her Dragon's Gift series draws upon her love of history and the paranormal elements that she can't help but include.

COPYRIGHT

Made in the USA
Columbia, SC
24 February 2019